The Journey of the Diva Pack

Book 1

Karen A. Cheeks

Copyright © 2014 Karen A. Cheeks

All rights reserved.

This book is a work of fiction. Any references or similarities to actual events, real people, living or dead, or to real locales are intended to give the novel a sense of reality. Any similarity in other names, characters, places and incidents is entirely coincidental.

ISBN-13: 978-1505867756
ISBN-10: 1505867754

DEDICATION

To every person who has ever had a dream … don't give up! Chase after your dreams.

To: Janet
Thank you for your support and friendship! Much love to you!

The Journey of the Diva Pack
Book 1

God bless and enjoy the book!

Karen A. Cheeks

www.karencheeks.com

Karen Cheeks

ACKNOWLEDGMENTS

I thank God for "stirring up the gift" inside of me. Without Him, I would not have been able to write this book.

To all the beautiful ladies in my life who are a part of my "diva pack," I thank you for your love, friendship, support and prayers! Everybody needs to be encouraged and loved unconditionally, and I appreciate you all from the bottom of my heart!

I must extend a special thank you to my proofreaders, Angela Burnside, Janine Harrigan and Michele Renee Woodfork. I appreciate each of you for taking the time to read the book and provide invaluable feedback.

Iris Lynn Skinner is a godsend. We started out as coworkers and became friends. I thank God for you, your heart and your encouragement through the years. Thank you for editing this book. You are the absolute best!

To my family, I love you to the moon and back! And last, but certainly not least, I want to thank my wonderful husband, Antonio Cheeks, for his love and support. You are always in my corner and you are my biggest fan. Love ya babe!

PROLOGUE

Laughter spilled into the hotel corridor as Desiree approached the door to the suite. Excitement was bubbling up inside of her. It had been six months since she had seen her best girlfriends.

She decided to try and sneak in the room and surprise the ladies. Quietly slipping the hotel key card into the lock, she waited for the light to flash green and opened the door. There was so much noise from the CD player and television that the other three ladies did not hear her enter the hallway of the suite.

"I wonder when Ray is going to get here. It's getting late," said Tiffany.

"You know our girl. She ain't never on time for nothing!" said Lauren. "She's just like one of my scrump-diddly-umptious pastries ... flaky." Desiree frowned at that statement.

Is that what Lauren really thinks about me? I know we're not the closest in the group, but "flaky"? She tried to come up with a witty comeback to announce her presence, but before she could open her mouth, Samantha chimed in.

"Scrump-diddly-umptious?! Girl, you are too funny! I

don't know if I would call Ray flaky, but sometimes she just has, umm, other priorities," offered Samantha. "That's my girl and I love her. I just wish she would put us before her career sometimes. I mean we only get together twice a year."

"Ya'll leave her alone. If I was a singer looking to get my big break, I would take last-minute gigs, too," said Tiffany. "I just hope she's all right. It's a little after midnight and driving in these mountains is no joke. I actually thought she might ride up here with us."

"Wellllll ... I'm glad someone is concerned about me!" announced Desiree. "Ray," all three ladies screamed and ran across the spacious living room to hug and kiss the fourth member of their "Diva Pack."

"Humph, I don't know if I should be mad or glad to see ya'll! I heard what you said about me being flaky," said Desiree in a teasing voice, as she was not one to really display hurt feelings or emotions.

"Girl, you know we didn't say anything about you that we wouldn't tell you to your face," said Lauren. "We weren't trying to be mean."

"We?" questioned Desiree.

"Ok, *I* wasn't trying to be mean. I was just making a joke about you being late," said Lauren. "You're not getting sensitive on me, are you?"

"No, not at all. I just figured I'd let you know what I heard, so we could clear the air," said Desiree. "But if you say you weren't trying to be mean, then I have to take you at your word."

"Yes, and I'm sorry if I hurt your feelings. I really wasn't being nasty," said Lauren. "Now, can we drop this silliness and move on?"

"Sure, let's forget all about it," said Desiree, even though in the back of her mind she was still troubled. A knock at the door broke up the conversation and Tiffany walked down the hallway to see who was interrupting their conversation. Desiree followed closely behind, and the other two went back into the living room. The bellman was on the other side of the door with five Louis Vuitton suitcases for Desiree.

"Oh, thank you! You can just set my luggage by the fireplace," said Desiree, pointing toward the living room. "Tiff, do you have any ones so I can tip the bellman? Unfortunately, I only have large bills. My ones were eaten up at the tolls," Desiree whispered.

Tiffany dug into her jeans pocket and handed Desiree five ones. With her accountant's mind, she was thinking if Desiree had planned out her money as meticulously as she did packing, she might not have to borrow so much and would manage her funds better!

By the time the bellman had unloaded the suitcases, Desiree was in full control again. "Thank you for bringing my luggage up here so quickly. Here's a little something for you," she said with a sly smile on her face. Desiree handed the bellman his tip and let her hand linger for just a moment.

"You're welcome ma'am," he said, as he blushed and his blue eyes became bashful. "Just let me know if you need anything else. By the way, my name is Brian."

"Byr–, oh Brian! I thought you said something else," Desiree said a little nervously. "I will let you know if we need anything else, sugar," she said while ushering him to the door. Tiffany looked on curiously at how Desiree switched from flirty to uneasy. Desiree looked at Tiffany's questioning eyes. "I know what you're thinking."

"Oh yeah? Well, this I've got to hear," said Tiffany drily.

"You want to know why I was flirting with that young boy!" said Desiree.

"Well, that did cross my mind," said a laughing Tiffany.

"Let me tell you something Sister Souljah, I stay open to everybody. I don't care if you are young, old, black, white, yellow, purple or green," said Desiree. "As long as you are a man, you're straight and you're fine, I'll talk to you! I just love men! Of course that doesn't mean I want anything serious, but I do like to get attention from men … all of them."

"Keep hanging with me Tiff, you'll learn a few things. Like how to …"

"What are you two talking about in the hallway?" asked Samantha. "Come on in the living room, so we can get this party started!"

"Ok Ray, you have five suitcases. Please tell me one of them has the wine," said Lauren.

"Girl, you know it. Heeyyy … I got white wine, red wine, sweet wine, strong wine, a little beer and … umm Tiff, you ok?" asked Desiree when she looked up and saw Tiffany was looking a little concerned. "Oh yeah, that's right! I forgot you gave up drinking. Well, I got some soda, too!"

Everybody laughed and Tiffany felt the tension leave her body. She had just rededicated her life to Jesus two months ago. She knew her girls were not in that same space. They were more like CME's … only attending church on Christmas, Mother's Day and Easter, but she hoped they would still be able to remain close despite her decision to make some changes in her life to glorify God.

As Mother Henderson told her, she might be the one to lead her friends to the Lord by being an example for them. She sure hoped so and she didn't want to slip up and fall back into her old partying ways by hanging out this weekend.

A subset of Black Greeks from Howard University, Morgan State University, Temple University, University of Maryland and Delaware State were hosting a Martin Luther King Jr., commemoration weekend at a beautiful ski resort in the mountains of Pennsylvania. This was their third year of bringing all nine of the historically Black Greek letter organizations together.

Tiffany, although not a Black Greek, had to hand it to them, they always did things in a classy way and made sure to provide some education along with the fun. There were workshops planned for entrepreneurs, networking, discussions on social issues, as well as live entertainment each night. If the sorority she was considering while in college had not been suspended, she probably would have pledged and been more in tune with Black Greek life.

Only Lauren and Samantha had pledged. One was an AKA and the other was a Delta, but the different sororities did not matter to the two ladies, they were closer to each other than to many of their sorors.

Desiree's voice broke Tiffany out of her thoughts. "Hey, let's get in our pajamas and get comfy before we pour the wine and catch up with each other," said Desiree. "Did you guys already choose rooms?"

"Yep, Lauren and I are over there and you and Tiffany are in the other room," said Samantha.

"Ok. Tiffany did you check both rooms? We better not have gotten the short end of the stick," said Desiree.

"Girl, you are always cutting up! This suite is gorgeous! The rooms are both really large, but I'm not sure if all of your clothes are gonna fit in the closet," said Tiffany jokingly.

"Mmm hmm, we'll see!" said Desiree. "Let's go change."

The ladies departed and kept talking in their rooms as they were changing. "Girl, I think one of my titties is bigger than the other one!" said Desiree. "Look!"

"I am not looking at your breasts," said Tiffany. "And why you gotta use the word 'titties' anyway?"

"Oh boy, you aren't gonna be censoring everything that comes out of my mouth now that you're a prude, are you?" asked Desiree.

"I'm not a prude!" said Tiffany. "I just don't like the word 'titties.'"

"Ok, what should I say then?" challenged Desiree.

"How about boobies or breasts?" said Tiffany sarcastically.

"Girl, bye!" said Desiree. "Just because you love Jesus does not mean that I am going to start changing my vocabulary. I keep it real."

Tiffany stayed silent and continued changing her clothes. The silence in the room was becoming uncomfortable, so she decided to break the ice by changing the topic.

"So, how's your singing career going?" asked Tiffany.

"I've been staying busy. My agent keeps lining things up for me, but I'm still waiting for my big break. You know, when I can get some national exposure," said Desiree. "As a matter of fact, when we all get back in the living room, I have some great news to share."

"Ooo, I can't wait. Let's go! I'll pull Lauren and Samantha out of their room."

Lauren was already sitting on the couch waiting for the others to join her. "Where's Samantha," Tiffany asked curiously.

"In the room, talking to her boo," said Lauren. "I think she was getting into an argument about coming up here for the weekend instead of spending it with him."

"He better stop playing! This is our time," said Desiree. "Have any of you met him?" Both Lauren and Tiffany shook their heads no. "Well then, he's a Johnny-come-lately. If we haven't met him that means he's not in yet and has no say in what Samantha does with her free time."

Just then, the girls heard something fall in the bedroom where Samantha was and ran in to make sure everything was alright. They found her lying on the bed crying and her phone smashed into tiny little pieces across the room.

"Sam, what is going on?" asked Lauren. After a couple of minutes of silence, Lauren went over and rubbed Samantha's back. "Are you ok?" Lauren asked softly.

Samantha held up her tear-filled face and shook her head no. "What did that fool say to you?" asked Desiree. "Do I need to call my cousin Pookie on him?" She was hoping to lighten the mood and make Sam laugh. Tiffany and Lauren chuckled, but stopped abruptly when Sam shook her head yes.

"Oh Lord!" said Tiffany.

"God ain't got nothin' to do with this! What did this idiot say to you?" demanded Desiree. She didn't mean to bark at Tiffany, but she was so furious with this guy. If he thought he could threaten her friend, he had another thing coming. The other three may have come from suburban backgrounds, but Desiree was from the streets and she knew about thug life.

"He said … he t-told me that if I didn't come home tonight, he was going to be waiting for me when I returned to make sure I never went anywhere ever again," said Samantha.

"What the hell is wrong with this guy?" asked Lauren. "I mean is he for real? Has he done something like this before? Has he ever hit you?" Lauren fired out the questions rapidly.

"No, he's never done anything like this," said Samantha. "The biggest thing he's ever done is start arguments when I would hang out with some friends after work, but that's about it. He's never threatened me before."

"Well, this is going to be his first and last time," said Desiree. "I would say let's call him back and tell him a thing or two, but your phone is done. By the way, why did you smash your phone?"

"I didn't want him to be able to reach me," said Samantha.

"Umm, you could have just turned your phone off," Tiffany said drily.

"Oh yeah, I guess you're right … duh," Samantha said weakly. The girls all laughed for a minute, relieved to see their friend start to come around.

"Come on ya'll, let's get a drink and relax in the living room," said Lauren. "We need a break from this drama. But we're going to help you figure out how to get that busta out of your life before this weekend is over."

"Lauren, I couldn't agree more!" Desiree said happily. "Besides, I have some great news to share with you guys."

"Tiffany, you have to get a glass of wine. C'mon we have to toast to Ray's good news!" Lauren teased her.

"Well, maybe one glass, but give me a ginger ale, too," said Tiffany. She had no intention of drinking the wine, but she would not tell the "Diva Pack" that or else it was going to be a long night arguing about her choice to leave the bubbly alone.

Lord, I didn't think it was going to be so hard to stand for You and my commitment to do things Your way. I thought my girls would understand and be more supportive, Tiffany pondered silently to herself.

"Ok, everybody raise your glass. Here's to a fun weekend with my girls!" Desiree said. "And guess wha-aat? Drum roll please …"

Tiffany started to do a pseudo drum roll on the coffee table. "I'll be singing for two of the evening shows … one by myself and one with that fine, sexy Joe Taylor," hollered Desiree.

Lauren, Samantha and Tiffany had disappointed looks on their faces. They wanted to be happy for Desiree, but not for something like this. "I thought this was our weekend to hang out and spend time together. How can all of us do that if you're off working and rehearsing for most of the weekend?" Samantha asked.

"Well, we have tonight and during the day on Saturday and Sunday. I will have to rehearse in the afternoon and then get prepared for the show," said Desiree. "But I thought you would be happy for me …"

"We are … I guess we're just seeing clearly that you have other priorities besides us," said Samantha.

"Yeah, I am happy for you, but I don't really feel much like celebrating right now," said Lauren. She and Samantha walked off and went back into their room.

"Do you feel that way too Tiff?" Samantha asked.

"Yeah, sort of, I mean I didn't think we had to do everything together, but this is going to take you away from us quite a bit," Tiffany answered. "I guess we just miss the closeness of the 'Diva Pack' and at least three of us were thinking this weekend would be the perfect time to get back on track."

"I think I'm going to turn in, too. I'll see you in the morning, if you're around," Tiffany said.

"Wow ... but I didn't even get to tell ya'll the best part. Because I'm working, this expensive suite will be covered by the Black Greeks. So, we get to stay here for free this weekend," Desiree whispered to herself.

A lonely tear escaped out of the corner of her eye, as she tossed back her glass of red wine. I will not allow them to get to me. This is my big break and if they can't support me in this, then maybe it's time for the "Diva Pack" to break up and go our separate ways ... the nerve of them!

⌘ Desiree ⌘

CHAPTER ONE

Desiree took one last look in the mirror before heading down to the lounge for her set. Her shoulder length hair was swept up into a loose curly updo that framed her heart-shaped face. The eye shadow made her eyes look smoky and seductive. Now if only her fake lashes would stay in place, she should be fine, Desiree thought.

Why did I not pick up that extra glue in my medicine cabinet? Oy vey! Oh well, I can't worry about that now. She continued to look at her outfit. Her little black dress was hugging every curve of her body and it stopped just above her knees. Her shimmery sheer stockings would glisten in the spotlight as everyone's eyes would be locked on her on stage …

The loud banging on the door broke through her reverie. Who in the world is knocking on the door! Don't they know I'm trying to get myself together? "What do you want," asked Desiree.

"Ray, you have been in there for two hours. I need to get ready for tonight also," said Tiffany.

"Oh sorry, I forgot about you," Desiree muttered.

Things had been pretty cold between the ladies all morning. No one was really talking to Desiree. So, she left early in the morning and decided to have some fun on her own until rehearsal. I can't believe how childish they are being, she thought.

"I'm just touching up my lips. I'll be out in a sec," Desiree said through clenched teeth.

Desiree added just a touch of peach gloss to bring out the natural color of her honey-colored skin. She slipped her size 8 feet into her red-bottom shoes and sauntered out the door.

"Wow! You look great," said Tiffany before she remembered that she was supposed to be mad with Desiree. Tiffany thought twice about her attitude and told her honestly, "I hope your show goes well tonight sweetie."

Some of the ice around Desiree's heart started to melt and she smiled briefly and headed out the door. She didn't want to admit it, but she had huge butterflies flitting around in her stomach. She was so nervous she decided not to eat much that day for fear of throwing up once she got on stage. Desiree walked a little wobbly down the corridor to the elevator. As she waited, she felt someone come alongside of her.

"Good evening," said a rather tall brother with beautiful chocolate skin, short dreadlocks and a perfectly trimmed goatee. He looked extremely fit in his charcoal slacks and maroon button-down shirt.

"Good evening," Desiree replied.

"May I escort you downstairs, Miss …" he inquired.

"Why, yes you may. And my name is Ms. Walker," Desiree answered coyly.

"Well, Ms. Walker, when will I have the privilege of learning your first name," he asked.

"Well, Mr. …"

"It's Julian. Just Julian," he replied.

"Ok then, Julian, when I get to see something truly

special from you, you'll find out my first name," Desiree said with a husky voice.

Just then the elevator doors opened and it was completely crowded. Julian told them that they would catch the next one.

"So, it looks like I have a few more minutes alone with you," said Julian.

"Yes, it does appear that way," Desiree said. She was enjoying this little game of cat and mouse. It was keeping her preoccupied and not focused on her nerves. "Let me ask you something …" her voice trailed off as her cell phone started to buzz.

"Excuse me for a moment," Desiree said to Julian.

"Hello. Oh hi, Kevin! I didn't recognize this number you were calling from.

What?! You're here! Oh, I'm so glad you made it, I didn't think you would get here until tomorrow!

Yep, I'm just waiting on the elevator to bring me downstairs.

Well, of course I look fabulous darling. I mean, come on now, tonight's a big night.

"Uh huh … what do you mean … I'd rather you tell me now … ok, fine. I will see you in a couple of seconds. The elevator just arrived."

Desiree hung up the phone and walked into the elevator, preoccupied by the conversation with her manager. Something just didn't feel right about this gig tonight. I knew I should have trusted my gut instinct and declined doing this, but Kevin convinced me it would be fine.

Desiree had forgotten all about Julian, but suddenly his piercing stare brought her back to the present. "Hey, hi, I'm sorry, I was lost in thought," Desiree confessed.

"It's ok. So, your man is meeting you downstairs?" Julian questioned.

"Kevin? Noooo … he's just my …" before she

finished her sentence, the elevator chimed and stopped on the 5th floor and a large group of fraternity "bruhs" got on. Desiree inched slightly closer to Julian, who gave the men a head nod, while putting his arm around Desiree and pulling her closely to his chest.

Oh my, why does this man smell soooo good and feel nice and solid. I've got to stay focused, but all I want to do is look into his beautiful eyes with those thick, long lashes and kiss the daylights out of him.

When the doors opened, Desiree wished she could have stayed in Julian's arms a little longer. But she reminded herself that she had a show to do and she couldn't get distracted. The "bruhs" politely let her and Julian get off first.

CHAPTER TWO

"There you are!" said Kevin, who seemed to be pacing back and forth in front of the elevator. "I was beginning to get worried about you. I should have come up here with you yesterday. Why are you traveling on the elevator by yourself anyway? Where are your *diva girlfriends*?"

"Kevin, don't start. Besides, this wonderful gentleman escorted me down," Desiree said. Kevin looked Julian up and down, grunted his appreciation and pulled Desiree away. She turned back to say sorry, but all she caught was the back of her handsome friend heading toward the bar.

"Kevin, that was rude!" Desiree hissed, barely controlling the anger rising inside of her.

"No, it wasn't. We have important business to discuss. You can flirt with your muscle-headed friend later," said Kevin.

"Don't go there with me! What's the update?" questioned Desiree. "Are they cancelling my show?"

"Not exactly ... they still want you to sing, but there

has been a slight change of plans," explained Kevin. "They got someone else to perform in the ballroom for the dinner celebration. So, you'll do your set in the bar where your man went."

"Oh, that's just peachy! So, I'll be singing to five people?" She didn't say all that was on her mind. *Why in the world did she let this idiot of a manager talk her into doing this last-minute gig. I should have just chilled with my girls ... and now they are mad at me.*

"Look, I'm sorry that it worked out this way," said Kevin. "I didn't know they were still looking for a headliner, uh uh ... I mean, a more well-known singer. But everybody didn't pay for a ticket to the dinner, so you should have a nice crowd in the bar."

"You betta hope so," Desiree said through clenched teeth. "Are there any changes for tomorrow night's performance?"

"As a matter of fact, there are," Kevin said with a sheepish grin.

"This is going from bad to worse," muttered Desiree.

"It's just that I thought you would be singing a couple of duets with Joe Taylor. But, as it turns out, he just wants you to be a background singer with two other ladies," said Kevin. "That's not so bad, honey. You'll still have your hotel room paid for and get a paycheck for filling in ... just not as much."

"What the ...! You know what ... I can't do this with you right now. I need to calm down before I explode," yelled Desiree. "Get away from me!"

The people in the lobby were staring at the arguing couple as Desiree stormed outside with her nostrils flaring. It looked as if steam were coming out of her ears. She didn't feel the frigid temperatures because her anger kept her heated. If she smoked, she probably would have lit a cigarette as she paced back and forth.

When I get back to New York, I am looking for a new manager. Kevin is full of crap! I'll never work with him again after this fiasco, Desiree declared to herself. I have enough talent to be the main act, and I will get there one day soon without Kevin.

"Miss, are you alright?" asked the gentle doorman.

"Yes, I'm fine. I just needed to get some fresh air," replied Desiree.

"It's quite cold out here. I don't want you to catch a cold," he said kindly.

"Thank you. I'll be fine," Desiree said curtly. She looked at the older gentleman and realized she had hurt his feelings. "I'm sorry ... I'm not in a very good mood right now. I should go back inside, I might mess up my voice and I need to sing two nights in a row," Desiree said smiling sheepishly.

Desiree walked back inside and bumped into Tiffany, Samantha and Lauren. They looked shocked to see her in the lobby. "Hey Ray! I guess we'll see you performing in the main ballroom in a few minutes," said Samantha.

"Umm, not tonight ... I'm singing in the bar," said Desiree. "Enjoy your evening. If it's not too late, maybe you guys can come to the bar and catch the end of my set?"

"Sure, if it's not too late," said Lauren. "Break a leg or whatever the phrase is nowadays."

"Yep, that's it. Thanks." Desiree said with a smile that didn't quite reach her eyes. She was so down and embarrassed that she didn't notice the look the other three women exchanged. Desiree walked toward the bar with a look of defeat about her.

"I don't feel sorry for her. That's what she gets for blowing us off. She should have stuck with our original plan," said Lauren.

"Sometimes, you can be so mean Lauren," Samantha scolded. "Yeah, she's wrong but I feel bad for her. I wonder how she ended up singing in the bar."

"Yeah, me too. I don't know about you, but I'm going to try and slip in there a little later to show her some support," said Tiffany.

"I think I will, too," Samantha chimed in and looked hopefully at Lauren.

"Hmm ... depends on how I feel," said Lauren, who was still a bit salty over Desiree's decision to work during their holiday vacation. Both Samantha and Tiffany looked at her with frowns.

"What? Don't give me that look! I said I'll see how I'm feeling by the end of the night. C'mon let's go to the big dinner celebration ... I wonder who's gonna be the main entertainment," said Lauren.

CHAPTER THREE

Desiree saw Kevin waiting for her in the doorway. She tried to compose her face and calm her nerves so that she could get through this humiliating setback.

"You cool off yet," asked Kevin. He hoped she would not blow this gig for him. He had a lot riding on Desiree not messing up his connections with the event organizers. If she walked away or screwed up, they could shut his management business down for good.

"I'm better, but you and I are going to talk about this when we get back to the city," said Desiree. "So, what's the game plan for this evening?"

Unbeknownst to Desiree, Julian was observing her interaction with Kevin. He liked what he saw and couldn't figure out why she was connected to that guy. They seemed like an odd couple. She was beauty and grace and he looked like a trickster. Julian didn't care for his shifty eyes or rude attitude either. And Julian couldn't figure out how he knew that guy or why he was getting worked up over this woman.

I don't even know her. Let me finish my drink and head over to the main event. As he threw the last remnants of his drink back, he noticed that she got up and went over to the piano. Well now, if she's going to sing, I want to stick around.

Julian ordered another cranberry juice. He had not touched an alcoholic drink in more than seven years, and had no intention of breaking his sobriety. Every now and then, he would test his resolve by going into a bar, but the horror of his former life, plus the 12-step program, was enough to keep him on the straight and narrow.

Desiree sat down at the piano and began to run her fingers over the keys. She closed her eyes and took a deep breath and began to play softly. My rehearsal with the band was all for nothing … it's just gonna be me tonight. Oh well, I can't think about that now.

The music soothed her fragile nerves as she began to sing. Her smoky, sultry alto voice caressed the words to "Forever, For Always, For Love."

Music had the ability to transport her to a place of peace. By the time the song ended, she felt confident and ready to get into her first set.

"How ya'll doin' tonight?" Desiree asked the crowd. By this time, there were about 15 people in the room. The crowd barely responded. "I said, how ya'll doin' tonight?" She heard a couple of "fine" and "good" responses.

"Well, all you fine and good people, my name is Desiree Walker. We are going to have some fun tonight. Is that alright?" Desiree told the small audience. "Is that alright?" she repeated. "YES," everyone shouted back.

"Oh that sounds so much better. Let's goooo!" Desiree liked to take her audience on a journey through music. She got started with Jill Scott's song "Golden," to warm up the crowd. Most people knew that song and they could sing the chorus with her, since she didn't have any backup singers.

After 45 minutes of singing, playing and bantering with the audience, Desiree's emotions were flying high. There was so much energy inside the bar that the crowd had grown to about 50 people. She decided to end the first set by taking folks back a few years with Heather Headley's song "He Is."

"Whew, I love that song!" said Desiree to thunderous applause. "Are ya'll having fun?"

"YES," everyone shouted.

"Alright, alright! We're gonna take a short break and come back for the second set. If you have friends who aren't in here, go get them! The second set is gonna be better than the first," shouted Desiree.

Kevin walked up to the piano and hugged Desiree. "Girl, you slayed them! I knew you would be great," he said.

"Thanks Kevin. Can you get some hot tea for me?" Desiree asked. He nodded and went to the bar.

Desiree was still reflecting on the good vibes coming from the audience and didn't notice when Julian approached the piano. "Well Ms. Desiree, you are full of surprises," said Julian.

"Hi there," she replied. "Did you enjoy the music?"

"Do you even have to ask? I am so impressed. You were absolutely wonderful. I couldn't take my eyes off of you," said Julian. "You are definitely a rising star."

"Aww, thank you!" said a slightly blushing Desiree.

Julian was surprised to see that she had a little bit of a shy side to her. He liked that about her. By this time, Kevin showed back up with her tea.

"Thanks Kevin. Let me introduce you to a new friend of mine. Julian, this is my manager Kevin. And Kevin, this is the gentleman who escorted me down here on the elevator," Desiree said with the intent of clarifying her relationship with Kevin. The two guys shook hands, but Desiree sensed that there was a bit of uneasiness in the atmosphere. *Oh well, nothing I can do about that.*

As she was sipping on her tea, a few admirers came up and talked to Desiree. She really loved the fan interaction. It always gave her a feeling of validation when she heard how the music touched them. One guy said he had been feeling depressed until the music lifted his mind away from his problems for a while. A young woman, named Susan, told Desiree that she and her friends didn't buy tickets to the dinner and thought that they would not have any entertainment. But Susan said she was so glad they got to see her and learn about a new artist.

"Do you have any CDs out yet," asked Susan.

"Not yet, I am working on my first CD and it should be ready in a couple of months," shared Desiree. "You'll get a sneak peak at some of my new songs in the second set."

"I can't wait," said Susan.

"Here's a flyer with my website. Be sure to sign up for my e-newsletter, which gives updates about my music and appearances," said Desiree.

"Ok, I will," replied her newest fan.

"So, you're working on your first CD," inquired Julian.

"Were you eavesdropping on my conversation," Desiree asked with a twinkle in her eyes. Julian just shrugged his shoulders, and did not answer the question. "Well, Mr. Nosy, yes I am working on my first project. I'm really excited about it."

"Do you do anything musically," asked Desiree.

"As a matter of fact, I do," he responded. "Maybe we can collaborate sometime."

"Yeah, maybe," Desiree said skeptically. "Well, I better get back to it. I see I now have a piano player joining me. I better bring him up to speed."

"Ok, I'll talk to you later," said Julian.

CHAPTER FOUR

The Diva Pack, minus Lauren, entered the bar midway through Desiree's second set. She was on the stage singing something original they had never heard before, but it sounded very fresh and soulful. Soon they were bobbing their heads along with everyone. It was standing room only in the bar at this point. Samantha and Tiffany tried to get as close to the stage as possible.

"Would you ladies like to sit down," a handsome man with short dreadlocks and goatee inquired.

"Oh thank you, yes, that would be nice," said Samantha. He and his friend got up from their table to allow the two women to sit and enjoy the rest of Desiree's show.

"Hey man, are you gonna sign this lady," asked Julian's friend Leonard.

"I think so. I've got to get her away from her manager first," said Julian. "I think he's the same guy that screwed over one of my other artists. I bet he's doing the same thing with Desiree and that's why she's singing in a bar instead of the main ballroom. But, if she'll let me, I'll fix all of that."

"Yeah, her sound is unique," said Leonard.

"I'm going to close out the evening with one of my favorite songs by the beautiful Ms. Etta James," said Desiree. Her husky voice slowly belted out the words to "At Last."

Desiree had been singing the ballad with her eyes closed. When she opened them at the very end of the song, she looked over at Julian's table, but only found her friends. Trying to hide her disappointment, she thanked the crowd for sharing their night with her. Her manager ran up on the stage and made a few announcements about Desiree's upcoming CD and mentioned that people should contact him for bookings.

Desiree felt like she floated off the stage as she sat on the side to reflect on the night. Now where did Julian go, she wondered. Several people started coming up to her to hug her and thank her for sharing her gift with them. Some wanted to take pictures, so they could post them on their social media pages. It was all a lot of fun to Desiree. But Julian was not very far from her thoughts.

Tiffany and Samantha finally made their way through the crowd. "Girl, you were so good," said Tiffany. "I'm really glad we got a chance to catch some of your show."

"I think you were better than the singer they had in the main ballroom. No disrespect to her, of course, but she must have been tired or something!" said Samantha.

Desiree was tickled by that compliment and almost fell out of her seat she laughed so hard. "Thank you, Sam!"

"Hey, where's Lauren?" asked Desiree.

"She went up to the room. She wasn't feeling well. In fact, she left us before the dinner celebration was over," said Tiffany.

"Yeah, that's right. Maybe we should go and check on her," said Samantha.

"I hope she's ok. You guys go ahead. I need to finish wrapping up a few things with Kevin, but I'll be up in a little while," said Desiree.

Once Desiree was sure the ladies had left the bar and were on the elevator, she picked up her cell phone and placed a call.

"Hey B!" said Desiree.

"Don't get your panties all in a bunch ... I know you don't wear panties," Desiree said drily to her friend's loud protest. *"I was making a funny."*

"Listen, I need a favor from you. Are you listening?" Desiree asked impatiently.

"Ok, my girl was threatened by some fool with an inferiority complex. So, I need you and your boys to scare the life out of him. I don't want him killed; just put the fear of God in him! You dig?"

"Cool. I'll call you back tomorrow or Monday with details about him. All I know right now is that he's in DC."

"Haven't you ever heard of giving someone a 'heads up'?" Desiree asked laughing at her friend. *"I'll talk to you later man."*

Desiree and B went way back to middle school. He was good friends with her brother and always looked out for her. She could always call on him when she needed something "fixed."

CHAPTER FIVE

As Desiree put her phone away, she felt someone's eyes on her. When she turned around, she saw that it was Julian staring at her from across the room. Desiree motioned for him to come over.

"I thought you had left for the evening," Desiree said looking pleased as punch that this fine brotha was still hanging around.

"No, I saw your entire show. I stepped out at the end to take a phone call," he responded.

"Well, what did you think?" Desiree asked curiously.

"I thought you were ... phenomenal," replied Julian. "In fact, I meant what I said. I'd love to work with you at some point, hopefully in the near future."

"Oh yeah? So, you work in this industry?"

Julian nodded in the affirmative.

"My manager says he knows everybody. It didn't seem like he knew you," Desiree questioned.

"I would humbly say that I am in a different league than your manager," said Julian. "He and I will never sit at the same table."

"Here's my card. Check me out when you have a moment," said Julian. "I heard you say you live in Harlem.

My office is there, too. So, when you're back in town, call my assistant and let's meet. Unfortunately, I have to head back tonight or else I'd offer to meet with you tomorrow."

"Ok, sure …" said Desiree skeptically. She wasn't sure who this arrogant man was, but he better recognize that she wasn't some second-rate act just willing to work with anybody. She'd check him out alright.

"I look forward to seeing you again. Have a good night," said Julian as he picked up her hand and kissed it gently. Desiree felt sparks shoot up and down her arm when his warm lips brushed against her skin. Maybe I won't be too hard on him with his sexy self, she thought. Hmm …

"Good night," Desiree said in her husky voice and gave him a mischievous smile.

Julian headed out and left Desiree dreaming about him. Kevin walked over and demanded to know what Julian wanted with her.

"What's it to you," asked Desiree.

"Do you know who that guy is?" shouted Kevin. Desiree looked puzzled. Kevin held up the card in Desiree's hand and she focused on the words.

"Oh … My … Goodness …" said Desiree.

"That's right. He's the president and CEO of SJC Entertainment," said Kevin. "He probably wants to sign you," he added dejectedly.

"Wait! Why do you sound disappointed?" asked Desiree.

"It's nothing. What did he say," Kevin asked again.

"He just said he would like to see me again," Desiree said vaguely. She knew Kevin was not always up front with her and she didn't feel the need to divulge the fact that Julian was also interested in working with her. After the fiasco this weekend, Desiree had no intention of keeping Kevin as her manager.

"I think he was just flirting with me," said Desiree. Kevin just looked at her suspiciously but didn't say anything else.

"How come you didn't tell me you knew him," asked Desiree.

"I don't know him. I met him a long time ago, but I didn't recognize him at first," said Kevin. "He didn't have those ugly dreadlocks before."

"Don't hate boo. It's not a good look on you," said Desiree. "I know you're hurting because you are losing your hair, but don't be mad at the brotha because he's got an abundance of hair on top of his head." She chuckled about Kevin's jealousy over hair.

"I'm not mad," said Kevin pouting.

"Whatever. Let's get back to Julian. So, what went down between you two," asked Desiree.

"I said it was nothing. I was representing this artist and he came along and stole her from me and blew up with his company," said Kevin. "He's a snake in the grass. Don't trust him."

"Yeah, I hear you," said Desiree as she slipped the business card out of Kevin's hand and into her little black purse.

"Well, it's getting late. What's my cut for tonight?" Desiree asked. Kevin handed her an envelope with cash inside. She counted the money and tried to remain calm.

"Kevin, where's the rest of my money. I know I am getting paid more than $250," said Desiree.

"Heyyyy, I had to pay the piano player and take my management fee, too," said Kevin.

"You know what? This is the last time you are going to get over on me," Desiree said with a deadly calm. "And guess what? I'm not singing back up tomorrow night! I'm going to enjoy myself with my girls like I planned to do. And you better not change a thing about paying for our suite, because if you do there will be hell to pay. Do you understand me?"

"Now, you listen to me you little b—," snarled Kevin.

"I would watch your language with the lady,"

interrupted Julian who just happened to be walking by the bar with his luggage on his way out.

"Lady, humph, she ain't no ..." the rest of Kevin's words were cut off when Julian grabbed him by the neck and lifted him off the ground.

"I don't know what the disagreement is about but I suggest you honor Ms. Walker's request," said Julian as he gave Kevin a strong shake and lowered him slowly to the ground.

Kevin was choking and sputtering and all Desiree could do was laugh. Julian motioned to his friend Leonard and whispered something in his ear before turning back to Desiree.

Julian held out his arm to Desiree and walked her out of the bar and to the elevator. "Don't worry, he won't bother you again. I'll see to that," he said.

"Oh, I'm not worried about Kevin. I was just getting ready to let him have it before you walked in," smiled Desiree. "He just better be glad you interrupted him because I was about to drop him to his knees."

Julian laughed at her spunk.

"It's funny because he and I were supposed to work on a new contract when I got back from this trip. But it doesn't look like I'll have to find the words to tell him that I'm moving on," said Desiree.

"That's great! Make sure you call my office as soon as you're back and settled," said Julian. "I've really got to run now, but I'll have a few choice words with your former manager before I leave."

"Thanks and be safe on the roads," said Desiree.

CHAPTER SIX

Desiree got into the elevator and smiled all the way up to the 15th floor. This may be the best thing that's ever happened to me. I might get a recording contract and a new man all at the same time. I can't wait to get back to New York!

Desiree put her key card in the door and walked into the suite to find all three ladies sitting in the living room looking worried.

All of Desiree's happy thoughts quickly evaporated into concern. "What's wrong?"

"We just found out that Lauren's pregnant," said Tiffany.

"Yayyyyy – Isn't this good news?" asked Desiree.

"… ummm, the father lives in Paris," added Tiffany.

"You mean Charles isn't the father?" said Desiree. "What are you going to tell your husband?"

"I don't knoooowwwwww," Lauren wailed and ran off into her bedroom.

After the ladies watched Lauren run into the room and shut the door, they turned back to each other and mouthed the word "WOW" silently.

"My mama always said, 'what's done in the dark will come to light,'" whispered Tiffany.

"Oh, I feel so bad for her," said Samantha.

"You've got to fill me in! Has she been having an affair?" asked Desiree.

"Not exactly. It seems that she and Charles have been at odds with each other for some time," shared Samantha. "Apparently, he lost his job at one point, and they have been fighting constantly. So, he became depressed or something."

"Hmmm … ok, so because of this situation, she stepped out on a brotha huh," questioned Desiree.

"Well, yes and no. Do you remember how she won an all-expense paid trip to Paris to participate in a pastry chef bootcamp," said Tiffany.

"Yeah, so?" replied Desiree.

"While she was there last month, she met a really nice, handsome French chef. She said they became friends during the bootcamp and helped each other out," said Samantha. "On the last night, they were drinking wine and talking and he told her about his wife and daughter who had recently gotten killed in a car accident."

"And while they were talking, he started to cry, so Lauren reached out and hugged him," chimed in Tiffany.

"Yeah, I think they were both feeling lonely and had been drinking wine. It seems that one thing led to another and they got busy," said Samantha.

"The real kicker, not that the other stuff isn't shocking, is that the next morning the chef tells Lauren that he'd had a vasectomy and she didn't have to worry about getting pregnant," Tiffany said.

"O.M.G. … this sounds like a movie, not real life," said Desiree. "Is she planning to keep the baby?"

"I think so," said Tiffany.

"Whoaa, I just thought of something. So, since this guy is French, is he also white?" asked Desiree.

"Yes," said Samantha.

"All hell is going to break loose when Charles sees that baby, if she doesn't tell him first," said Desiree. "As dark skinned as he is, there ain't no way in the world he's gonna believe it's his child."

"I know, it's about to get crazy for her. We just have to make sure that we are there to help support her through this time," said Samantha.

Desiree just nodded her head and began to think about how snooty Lauren could be sometimes. This new development in her life will certainly knock her down a few pegs. Oh, how the mighty fall, Desiree thought with a slight smile.

"What are you grinning about," asked Samantha.

"Nothing, I just started thinking about my evening and the wonderful man I met tonight," Desiree lied.

"Oh, do tell," said Tiffany.

"Well, I bumped into him on my way down for my show and he stayed around to listen," shared Desiree. "And get this, he owns SJC Entertainment and he's interested in working with me!"

"Oh, that's so great Ray! I'm really happy for you," said Samantha.

"That is some good news! What does he look like," asked Tiffany.

"He is tall, dark and handsome ... oh, and he has short dreadlocks and a nicely groomed goatee," gushed Desiree.

"He sounds like the guy who gave up his seat so Sam and I could sit down," said Tiffany.

"You know what, that's right! You guys were sitting at the table he had been at," said Desiree. "Isn't that funny?"

"It's a small world, I tell ya," said Samantha.

"Speaking of a small world ... I called a friend of mine who lives near DC and told him about your romantic situation," said Desiree. "We go way back and he'll do anything for me. So, I told him I would give him a few more details after I talked to you."

Samantha's eyes grew big as she looked at Desiree.

"What type of info do you need? And what's your friend going to do?" she asked.

"The less we know, the better. Of course, he won't kill the guy," said Desiree. "He'll just scare him a little bit and make sure he never bothers you again. So, I just need his name, address and phone number. We can leave the details up to my friend."

"Oh Ray, I don't know about this," said Samantha.

"Girl, are you planning to go back to that idiot?" asked Desiree.

"No! I just don't want him hurt. I do care about him," said Samantha.

"Well, the threat he made against you does not sound like he cares if you get hurt or not. In fact, he seems ready to hurt you himself," said Desiree.

"Ray's right, you can't sit there and do nothing. His threat sounded serious," said Tiffany. "But if you don't want to involve her friend, you at least need to get a restraining order right away."

"You're right. As soon as I get home, I will file a restraining order with the police," said Samantha.

"Good, we don't want anything to happen to you. Grown adults should not be making threats against anybody … that's just childish," said Tiffany.

"Yeah, I agree. But if that restraining order doesn't work, let me know and I'll have my boy handle it," said Desiree. "I've seen restraining orders fail one time too many."

Samantha nodded her agreement and got up to go to bed. "I'm getting sleepy. I'll see ya'll in the morning. Good night."

"Good night," Tiffany and Desiree said in unison.

⌘ Tiffany ⌘

CHAPTER SEVEN

Both Tiffany and Desiree had settled into their beds and were getting ready to drift off to sleep when Desiree's phone buzzed.

"Aww, hell naw," said Desiree after picking up her phone and reading a text message.

Tiffany really didn't want to ask what was wrong. She'd had enough drama for the night. But Desiree was still mumbling to herself and she knew she would never get to sleep until she shut up.

"What's the matter?" inquired Tiffany.

"Girl, I need a favor," said Desiree.

"What's up?" said Tiffany.

"Is there enough room in the car for me to ride back with the three of you," asked Desiree.

Tiffany wondered why Desiree needed a ride. "I thought you drove up here. What happened to your car?" she asked.

"Well, what had happened was …" said Desiree chuckling. But Tiffany did not find the joke funny, at all.

"You said you spent all your ones on tolls driving up here and then bummed $5 off of me last night," Tiffany snapped. "So, why is it that you now don't even have your car?"

"Girl, I'll give you your $5 back. Geez!" said Desiree.

"It's not about the money. I don't like being lied to," said Tiffany.

"Sorry, hun. I didn't mean to lie to you," said Desiree. "I was just trying to keep this situation quiet."

"But it looks like it's catching up with me," she added. "I rode up here with Byron and he was supposed to be taking me home, but his kid was rushed to the emergency room ... asthma, I think."

"Wait a minute ... you and Byron traveled up here together. Is this the same Byron we know from college? The same Byron that got married a few years ago? That Byron?" asked a heated Tiffany.

"Yes, it's the same one," said Desiree. "So what? We kick it every now and then."

"When you say, 'kick it,' do you mean that you two are still having sex?" asked Tiffany.

"Look, we're friends," said Desiree. "We have an understanding. We like to have a little fun from time to time when it's convenient for both of us. Besides he was my first and I always had a weak spot for him."

"You are setting yourself up for a serious disaster," said Tiffany. "I can't believe you don't have any respect for their marriage ... or how about yourself."

"This is going to come back to bite you," Tiffany continued. "The Bible says, we reap what we sow."

Desiree didn't say anything else. Tiffany was fuming. Both of my girls are living scandalous lives. I feel sorry for Lauren, after all that was a one-time mistake and she had been drinking. But Desiree has been carrying on with her foolishness for years! Didn't she have any respect for herself? She's always talking about not taking any crap from a man and standing on your own two feet. Yet, here she is taking leftovers from a man who will never be hers. Unbelievable!

"What?" asked Desiree.

Tiffany didn't realize she spoke her last thought out loud. "Nothing, it really doesn't matter," she mumbled.

"Look Tiff, I know you are mad and disappointed in me. That's why I didn't say anything," said Desiree. "In all honesty, I'm a little disappointed in myself. But for real, I don't know what it is about Byron but when he calls me, I just can't say no."

After pausing and thinking for a moment, Tiffany mumbled, "Umph, that sounds like a soul tie."

"A what?" asked Desiree.

"A soul tie," repeated Tiffany. "It's when an emotional bond or connection is formed with another person. It can be positive or negative, but you become bound to that person through your soul. So, for example, on the positive side, when a man and a woman get married, the Bible talks about the two becoming one flesh. Another way to look at it is their souls are knit together, usually through sex, love and mutual respect. However, the negative side of soul ties is when you engage in a relationship not ordained by God, you essentially open yourself up to a form of bondage to the other person. Even if that relationship ends, the connection does not go away immediately and that person has the ability to manipulate and control you or vice versa."

"Whoa, that's deep," said Desiree. "I can't have this conversation right now. I need to give this some thought."

"Ok, I understand. We can talk again when you are ready," said a yawning Tiffany. "Let's try and get some sleep. Good night,"

"Good night," replied Desiree.

Lord, please forgive me for being so judgmental. I know Desiree is wrong and she knows she is wrong. I should not have come at her like she was messing around with my man. I just never thought she would do something like this. Besides, it seems like she just met Mr. Wonderful tonight. Are you going to bless her with a great guy even though she's being trifling? Lord, I just don't get it.

It's not for you to understand. My ways are not your ways and My thoughts are not your thoughts. Just be there for her. She's going to need you. She's going to go through some tough times. Declare My truth, but do it in love.

I hear you Lord. I will. On another note, will Chris and I get back together?

Only trust Me.

I do, but I was hoping for a more specific answer, like yes or no.
Umm, hello … God? Did you hear me?
Oh, so you gonna be like that, huh? Ok, I will not ask you again. You just want me to trust you. Sometimes, you can be so frustrating! Nevermind, please forgive me Lord. I think I better go to sleep before I say something really crazy.

CHAPTER EIGHT

Bzzz. Bzzz.

Bzzz. Bzzz.

What is that noise? I peeked out from under the covers to see what insect was disturbing my wonderful dream about Morris Chestnut. When I find that little creature, I'm gonna smash it and go back into the arms of Mr. Chestnut.

As I looked around, I noticed Desiree was not in her bed, but her phone was lit up and started buzzing again. Why can't she just put her ding dang phone on silent? That's what a considerate roommate would do. What time is it anyway?

Hmmm, it's only 8:00 am. Let me turn her phone off, so I can get my last hour of sleep.

"Good morning sleepy head! Oh did my phone disturb you?" asked Desiree.

"Mmm hmm," mumbled Tiffany. It more than disturbed me, it woke me up, she thought to herself.

"I should have taken it with me to the gym. I had to get my morning work out on," said a cheery Desiree. "You should get into the habit of working out Tiff, it really helps to clear your head before you start your day."

"I just need a nice cup of coffee to get my day started,"

said Tiffany. "I was just about to turn your phone off so I can get my last hour of sleep."

"Oh, I'll change it to silent so you don't hear it buzz," said Desiree. "But you should get up so that we can get going."

"Ok, give me a few minutes and I'll get up," said Tiffany.

"Great, I'm going to take my shower now," said Desiree.

"Ok," said Tiffany, while crawling back in the bed. A few more minutes won't hurt. By the time Desiree gets out the shower, I'll go and get myself together, Tiffany thought to herself as she slowly drifted off into la-la land.

"TIFF –AN – EEEE" yelled Desiree in Tiffany's ear.

"Aaaa, what is wrong with you," screamed Tiffany as she shot straight up in the bed.

Tiffany looked over and didn't understand why Desiree was laughing so hard. "What is your problem," she snapped.

Desiree was wiping her eyes at this point, while chuckling to herself. "Girl, you should see the look on your face. It's priceless!" said Desiree.

"I think this is the last time that we are going to share a room together," said Tiffany through clenched teeth.

"Oh boo! You don't know how to take a joke," said Desiree. "I let you sleep an extra 45 minutes. But now it's time to get up so that we can make the most of this wonderful day."

"I know how to take a joke, but there's a time and a place for everything," mumbled Tiffany. And if Desiree wasn't off doing her own thing these last two days, we would have had plenty of time together. But Tiffany decided to keep her thoughts to herself. God told me to be nice, but this chick is testing my patience. She knows I am not a morning person!

"You can stop mumbling under your breath," said a laughing Desiree. "I'll leave you alone for a few minutes, so you can pull yourself together. I'll even bring you a cup of coffee, and hopefully that will help you start to function."

She just doesn't know. Me and Morris were about to get it on. With a heavy sigh, Tiffany stumbled into their bathroom and hopped into the shower.

CHAPTER NINE

After a hearty breakfast of omelets, waffles and fresh fruit, the ladies decided to check out the workshop on Black America's next generation of leaders. The panel discussion really zeroed in on how to prepare the next generation and what can be done to pave the way now. At the conclusion of the discussion, the audience gave the panel a standing ovation.

"Oh that was so good! I'm going to go up and talk to the teacher for a moment. I'll be right back and then we can head out for lunch," said Tiffany.

"Ok," said the Diva Pack in unison.

"I wonder if Tiffany knows the teacher. It looks like they are having an intense conversation," said Samantha, a few minutes later.

"I know. It's not like her to go up and introduce herself to complete strangers," said Lauren.

"Hmm ... maybe our little girl is growing up," Desiree joked. All three ladies were chuckling, as they noticed Tiffany making her way back.

"Are ya'll cuttin' up?" asked Tiffany.

"Who us? Of course not! So, what was that about? It looked like a heavy conversation," asked Samantha.

"I'll tell you about it over lunch," said Tiffany.

After the ladies were seated in the hotel restaurant, Tiffany began to share her thoughts.

"So, I think I want to switch my career," she said.

"Really, to do what?" asked Lauren. "Surely, you don't want to be a teacher."

"As a matter of fact, I do," said Tiffany. "I've been thinking about this a lot and I think it's time for me to make that transition. I hate working for an accounting firm. I make good money and everything, but there's more to life than that."

"But I thought you loved your job," said Samantha.

"I really like some of my co-workers, but I don't love accounting. I love what it affords me to be able to do, like travel, buy nice clothes, my car and house. But I hate the work. It's so boring to me!" shared a frustrated Tiffany.

"Well, I support you. I'm all for people following their heart," said Desiree.

"Thanks, I never wanted to go into accounting, but my mother discouraged me from following my passion for teaching and kids," said Tiffany.

"I never realized you wanted to be a teacher! Why did your mother discourage you from going that route?" asked Samantha.

"It's funny that you didn't realize I wanted to be a teacher, considering how much I volunteer to help with tutoring kids and whatnot," said Tiffany.

"A lot of people serve as tutors, but it doesn't mean they actually want to be a teacher," said Samantha. "Now stop avoiding my question! What's the deal with your mom?"

"Well, since you asked ... when my parents and I were looking for a college, I indicated that I wanted to go to a university that had a good school of education since I wanted to teach. My mother told me that there wasn't any good money in teaching. She went on to say that I might not get married, so I needed to make as much money as possible, so that I could take care of myself. And that, my friends, is why I chose to follow a career in accounting," Tiffany said bitterly.

"I agree with your mother," said Lauren.

All three women glared at her. "What did I say? She is right, there's no money in teaching!" Lauren added.

"We're just going to pretend that your pregnancy hormones have clouded your hearing and your judgment," said Desiree.

"Tiff, I'm really sorry to know that your mom said something so hurtful to you," said Samantha.

"It's ok. I know she wasn't trying to be mean. I think it was her way of looking out for me, since I don't have her beauty," said Tiffany.

"Girl, are you sure you weren't adopted. I don't mean no harm, but your mom says some crazy things to you. Your dad seems cool and everything, but your mom … she's kind of suspect," said Desiree. "What's up with her? Have you two ever gotten along?"

Tiffany sighed and fought back tears. "I used to wonder that too, except that I look just like my dad and I have my mother's light complexion. She and I have never had a close relationship and I don't know why," said Tiffany.

Samantha and Desiree both wrapped their arms around Tiffany as she shed a few tears. "Thanks, I'm going to go to the bathroom and fix my face. I'll be back in a few," said Tiffany.

After Tiffany walked away Desiree lit into Lauren. "What the hell is wrong with you? Why would you say that you agree with her mother?"

"I was only referring to the part about teaching. You don't make much money as a teacher," said Lauren.

"But did you hear the part about WHY her mother thought she'd be better at something else other than teaching?" asked an irritated Desiree.

"Yes and no. I wasn't focusing on that part," replied Lauren.

"If you weren't pregnant, I think I might just slap you," said Desiree.

"You are such a thug," said Lauren.

"Oh you think I'm a thug. I'll show you a thug," said Desiree.

"Ladies, calm down!" said Samantha. "Let's not do this here or now or ever!"

As Desiree and Lauren continued to lash at each other, Tiffany returned to the table. "What are you two arguing about now," she asked.

"Nothing," they both said at the same time.

"It must be something, it looks like fire is about to shoot out of Desiree's eyes," said Tiffany chuckling.

"It's really nothing," said Desiree. "So, let's get back to you. What's your game plan?"

"The reason I went to talk to the teacher, I wanted to get her thoughts about transitioning into the teaching profession," said Tiffany. "She was really helpful. Schools need a lot of STEM teachers and since I am a math whiz, there are all types of programs available to help prepare me for the classroom."

"Umm ... what is a STEM teacher," asked Lauren.

"It stands for science, technology, engineering and mathematics teachers. Apparently, there is a shortage in these subject areas," replied Tiffany.

"Oh, I see. I knew that but didn't know they were called STEM teachers," said Lauren.

"Well then, you didn't know," Desiree said sarcastically.

"Whatever Ray!" said Lauren.

"Don't say another word Ray. Leave it alone," said Samantha.

I'm not sure what transpired between Desiree and Lauren while I was in the bathroom, but I sure am enjoying the fireworks between those two. "Can you guys just call a truce and let's enjoy the rest of our day together," said Tiffany with a chuckle under her breath.

CHAPTER TEN

After another day and a half of laughter, dancing, eating, joking and meeting new people, the MLK weekend was coming to an end. The Diva Pack piled into the SUV to travel to Philadelphia where they would split up to head back to their respective homes.

"Hi daddy," said Tiffany, who called her parents after getting settled in her house.

"How was your trip," he asked.

"Well, you know how we do it!" said a giggling Tiffany. "We had a good time, there was never a dull moment."

"That's great sweetheart," said Jim. "Did you get on the slopes?"

"Daddy, you know I'm a snow bunny," said Tiffany. "The closest I got to the slopes was through a nice horse-drawn carriage ride with warm blankets and seat warmers to keep us toasty."

Tiffany was enjoying joking with her dad until he abruptly changed the topic. "Your mother just walked in, do you want to say 'hi' to her?" he asked.

"I guess so," replied Tiffany.

"Hi Tiff," said Mary.

"Hello Mother," answered Tiffany.

"How was your trip," she asked.

"Oh, you know, it was the same ole', same ole'," answered Tiffany.

"Hmm ... well, when are you coming home for a visit," Mary asked.

"Mother, I don't live at your home anymore. Philadelphia is my home now," Tiffany said in a huff.

"Why do you have to be so difficult? You know what I'm asking you," snapped Mary.

"I don't know. Maybe I'll come up in a few weeks," said Tiffany. "Hey, I've got to go. Desiree is still here and we need to pick up dinner before it gets too late."

"Ok, we'll talk to you later then," said Mary.

"Sounds good. Tell daddy that I love him. Bye," said Tiffany and hung up without waiting for a reply.

"Hey Tiff, I wasn't really eavesdropping, but you were pretty short with your mom. I mean you had a completely different tone talking with her than your dad," said Desiree.

"Yeah, we've never really been on the best terms, but it's gotten worse lately. Hopefully, we will work it out one of these days," said Tiffany.

"Well, don't wait too long. You don't want anything to happen and you haven't had a chance to clear the air or settle your disagreement," said Desiree.

"Speaking of clearing the air ... Ray, I'm really glad you are going to spend the night and head back to the city in the morning," Tiffany hesitated as she said, "... It gives us a little more time to talk."

"Girl, you think I don't realize you changed the subject," said a laughing Desiree. "But it's ok, it is cool that we get to spend some more one-on-one time together. Did you want to talk about something in particular?"

"As a matter of fact, I do," said Tiffany, as she took a deep breath. "First, I want to apologize for the other night when you shared what was going on with you and Byron. While I'm not condoning that relationship, I didn't mean to be so harsh and judgmental. I just want the best for you and that type of relationship is no good ... for either of you."

"Thanks for the apology, but in all honesty, it's none of your business," said Desiree.

"Oh, don't try and get brand new on me Ray!" said Tiffany. "We get in each other's business all the time. It's what we do! Plus you told me what was happening. It's not like I asked you. You volunteered this information." I stared at Desiree for a minute and then turned to look out the window before I said something I would regret later.

Calm down ... don't allow her attitude to get you off track.

Lord, I'm trying but she is not making this easy.

Show love.

I really didn't want to look at Desiree, but I had to try one last time to get her to see that she didn't have to settle for less. "Listen Ray, I didn't mean to snap at you. I'm just concerned. Do you get what I'm saying?" asked Tiffany.

"Yes, I do. But don't start preaching and going on about them soul ties. I told you, I needed to think about what you said," shared Desiree. "I know this relationship is not good, but I am not sure I want to get out. It's convenient for me, you know?"

"No, what do you mean by that?" asked Tiffany.

"I mean that I am a struggling artist right now, and Byron helps me out financially, and if he has a little itch, I don't mind scratching," said Desiree. "It's a win-win situation for both of us."

"Oh, I see," said Tiffany. Lord, what do I tell her?

The truth.

"What is that supposed to mean?" snapped Desiree.

"Calm down Ray. I'm just saying that I understand why you think this arrangement is working. I know you don't want me to preach, but can I share one thing that I feel in my heart?" said Tiffany.

"Sure, go ahead," sighed Desiree.

"I believe God will provide. All we have to do is ask Him. Sometimes we look for our answers in people and we don't ever think to take our problems to God," said Tiffany. "He wants to hear from us and be in relationship with every person on this planet. Whenever I have a need … financial or otherwise … I talk to the Lord about it. Do you know that He always makes a way for that need to be met? Now, I'm not going to lie and say that every situation worked out the way I wanted it to, but it worked out in a way that was best for me."

Lord, I can't tell if she is getting this. She's just looking at me.

Ask her.

"Does that make sense to you Ray?" Tiffany asked gingerly.

"I suppose, but it seems like you gave up everything you used to do for your religion. I don't want to give up my life. I love singing and sex," said Desiree.

"I have not given up my life. I love my life. I'm at peace and I finally have the courage to pursue my passion as a teacher. A relationship with God is not about do's and don'ts. The closer you get to Him, the more you want to please Him. For me, some of the things I used to do and places I used to go, I don't have a desire for anymore," said Tiffany. "As far as your singing, I don't know what God will say. You have to ask Him. But there are plenty of Christians who are also R&B singers."

"Ok, well what about sex?" demanded Desiree.

"I was coming to that. The main thing is God has

standards. And He put those standards in place to protect us from harm. According to His word sex is best enjoyed when you are married," said Tiffany. "One of the wonderful things about God is that He doesn't force His will on anybody. You can choose to do things your own way, but just be prepared to accept the consequences for not doing things His way."

"That sounds scary," said Desiree.

"I wasn't trying to be scary. I just want you to be aware that there are consequences when we purposely choose to go against the standard that God has set," said Tiffany. "I've disobeyed God many times, and dealt with the consequences. But I'm so glad that He gave me another chance. And He'll do the same for you, too."

"Tiff I hear you, but this is getting too heavy for me. I tell you what, the next time I come down, I'll go to church with you," said Desiree. "Deal?"

"Deal," said Tiffany.

All of a sudden both of their cell phones started to buzz at the same time. "It must be Sam and Lauren letting us know they are back," said Tiffany. "I'm going to look for a menu to order some food. Let me know what the girls say."

"OMG! Tiff come in here right now!" yelled Desiree a few moments later.

"Lauren sent two text messages. One is a video of Sam's crazy boyfriend smashing her car windows out with a baseball bat. The other message says they are at the police station filing a report and getting a restraining order," said Desiree.

"What in the world! This guy must be delusional," said Tiffany. "Try to call Lauren."

"I can't get through," said Desiree. "They must be talking with the police now."

"Unbelievable ... I need to eat, I can't think straight," said Tiffany. "Here, take a look at the menu. Hopefully, the girls will be able to talk by the time our food arrives."

CHAPTER ELEVEN

"Come on Ray, I have to be at work in 45 minutes. If you want me to drop you at the train station, we need to leave NOW!" shouted Tiffany.

"I'm coming. I just needed to finish my makeup. You never know who I'll meet on the train," replied Desiree.

"Oh Lord," mumbled Tiffany.

"What was that?" inquired Desiree.

"Oh nothing," said Tiffany. "Let's hit it!"

Both women were fairly quiet in the car lost in their own thoughts about what was happening in Washington, DC, with their friend Samantha.

"I'm so glad Lauren was with Sam last night," said Tiffany. "She must have been terrified."

"Yeah, I was so mad I was tempted to call my boy. But since they went to the police, I didn't want to get him involved," said Desiree.

"The good news is she can stay with Lauren for a little while, at least until she feels comfortable going back to her place," said Tiffany.

"Once they lock him up, Sam should be fine," said

Desiree. "At least I hope so. Have you noticed she seems to have a knack for picking losers?"

"Yes, I have noticed. Unfortunately, she has not found a good guy to treat her right," said Tiffany. "But this dude is the worst one."

"Indeed," said Desiree.

Both became quiet again as the music from the smooth jazz station filled the car. Tiffany was driving on auto-pilot and almost missed the exit to the 30th Street Station. "Oh shoot," Tiffany said under her breath while she whipped the car across two lanes and onto the exit ramp.

"Did you just cuss," asked Desiree.

"No, I said shoot," said Tiffany.

"Hmmm, it sounded like something else," said Desiree. "But I know Miss High and Mighty wouldn't dare dream of cussing."

"Girl, please hush before I miss my next turn. I don't have time to be playing with you," Tiffany said teasingly. She was not going to take any of Desiree's jabs seriously. She realized that Desiree was boxing with God and not her.

"Here we are," said Tiffany. "Let me pop the trunk and then I'll help you get your bags out of the car."

"Hey Tiff, I know I give you a hard time sometimes, but I'm really glad for your friendship," said Desiree. "Keep praying for a sista."

"You know I will," said Tiffany. "Now, let's get going so you can catch your train and I can get to work."

Tiffany and Desiree hugged and made promises to do a conference call later in the week to check on Samantha.

When Tiffany got back in the car, she had a missed call from Mother Henderson. Hmm, I wonder why she is calling me this morning. We normally don't chat until Tuesday evening. I hope everything is ok. I better call her now. Who knows what interesting problems will be waiting for me when I get to the office.

"Hi Mother Henderson, I just saw that you called me.

Are you alright?" asked Tiffany.

"Chile, I'm fine. I was checking on you. Are you alright," she replied.

"Yes, I'm fine. Why do you ask," said Tiffany.

"Did you talk to your parents when you got back home?" asked Mother Henderson.

"Yes, I talked to them for a little bit. They sounded like their normal selves. Is there something going on at the church?" inquired Tiffany.

"Maybe you should call your parents back and check with them," said Mother Henderson. "It's better you hear this news from them."

"What the ..." Tiffany had to stop and compose herself. She almost forgot who she was talking to. "Mother Henderson, why are you being so close-mouthed? You've got me thinking that something is terribly wrong."

"Nothing that can't be fixed with the help of the Lord, baby," replied Mother Henderson. "Call your parents tonight. I don't know why they didn't say something when you talked to them yesterday."

"Well, maybe because my friend Desiree was at my house. My mother kept asking me when I was coming home for a visit, but I kind of blew her off," said Tiffany.

"You and your mother will be sorting your relationship out soon," said Mother Henderson.

"Did the Lord tell you that," said Tiffany hesitantly.

"Not exactly, just an inkling I have," she answered. "Are you close to your job sweetheart?"

"I'm not too far away," said Tiffany.

"Alright, let's pray tomorrow night. One of my grandchildren has a recital tonight, so I will probably get home late," said Mother Henderson.

"That's fine with me. I'll talk to you tomorrow," said Tiffany.

"Sounds good! Have a blessed day," said Mother Henderson before the call disconnected.

Now that was weird. Mother Henderson was like her

adopted grandmother but Tiffany did not like the way their conversation just went. Mother Henderson had been in her life since she was a child, and it felt wrong to call her out, but that conversation left a bad taste in her mouth.

I wonder what could be going on at my father's church that would have an impact on my life in Philly. This day just keeps getting stranger by the minute.

CHAPTER TWELVE

When Tiffany got home at 6:30 pm, she kicked off her heels at the door and started pulling off her work clothes as she headed into her bedroom. She was so tired, she decided to lay down for a few minutes before figuring out what she would eat for dinner.

When she opened her eyes, she didn't realize that an hour had gone by. *I must have been really tired.* She padded into the kitchen and looked into her fridge. *Oh thank you Lord, I have leftover Chinese food. I forgot!*

Tiffany popped the food in the microwave as she reflected on her call with Mother Henderson this morning. *What in the world was she getting at? Well, the only way to find out is to call my parents and see what they have to say.*

Tiffany picked up the kitchen phone and dialed her parents' number.

"Hello," answered a feminine voice. Tiffany shuddered when she heard her mother on the other line. *I was hopping daddy was going to answer the phone. Oh well.*

"Hello Mother," said Tiffany.

"Hi there, I thought it was you but I didn't think you would be calling us back so soon," said Mary.

"Well, it's nice to hear from you too," said Tiffany sarcastically. "I can't do anything right, either I don't call enough or now I'm calling too much."

"Tiff, that's not what I meant. Do you have to blow everything out of proportion," said Mary. "I just don't know why you snap at everything I say to you."

Why hold back my thoughts and feelings. Mother Henderson and Desiree said we need to clear the air, well, maybe now is the time. "Maybe, it's because I don't believe you love me," said Tiffany. "You always criticize me, and I don't feel like you like me that much. I don't even know why. If you didn't want me, why did you have me?"

There was silence on the other end of the phone for a long time. "Is that what you think that I don't love you?" questioned Mary.

"That's what I said. You don't act like a mother who loves her child and you never have," said Tiffany. "It's like you are just doing your duty or something."

"Why you ungrateful little witch!" yelled Mary. "This is the thanks you are giving me for taking you in?"

"What are you talking about ... taking me in?" asked Tiffany in a hushed voice.

"What? That's not what I said," said Mary.

"That most certainly is what you said. What do you mean?" Tiffany said very calmly.

"Tiffany, I don't know what you are talking about," said Mary. "You misunderstood me."

Ping. The microwave alerted Tiffany that she had food warming up and it broke through her obsessive thoughts toward her mother.

"Is Daddy there," Tiffany asked quietly.

"No your father had a meeting at the church tonight," said Mary. "Do you want me to have him call you when he gets home?"

"Yes, that would be good. I'm going to eat my food," said Tiffany.

"Ok, honey," said Mary. "Tiffany, I'm sorry things got

a little heated between us. I want you to know that I do love you, I always have. I'm sorry that you don't feel my love."

"Ok," said Tiffany. "I'll talk to you later then." Tiffany didn't believe her mother and she was going to get to the bottom of the statement her mother yelled before coming back to her senses.

After that conversation, Tiffany's appetite was gone. She just picked through her food and ended up throwing most of it away. I sure hope my father calls me back soon. I've got a lot of questions that need to be answered. Oh yes, I do …

⌘ Samantha ⌘

CHAPTER THIRTEEN

"Aaagh!" Samantha jumped out of the bed abruptly awakened from the crazy nightmare she had been having. Still disoriented, she looked around the strange room and tried to remember where she was. Slowly her mind began to register that she was in Lauren's home. Samantha turned on the lamp and looked for her suitcase. She must have been running in her sleep because her clothes were drenched in sweat.

After changing into some dry night clothes, she headed toward the kitchen to get a glass of water. *I feel like a blind person in this house. I don't know where the light switches are.* As she felt along the wall hoping to find a switch, she inadvertently knocked a painting off the wall.

"Oh shoot!" said Samantha. "Now, what was that?" *I sure hope I don't wake Lauren with all this noise I'm making.* Just then light flooded the living room.

"Charles is that you?" asked Lauren.

"No, it's me Lauren," replied Samantha.

"Oh, what are you doing up at this time of night," asked Lauren.

"I had a nightmare and decided to get some water," said Samantha.

"Oh no, was it about Damon?" asked Lauren.

"Yes," Samantha quietly replied.

"Do you want to talk about it?" asked Lauren.

"Girl, I was just reliving the night that we came back from our trip. The only difference was that I was inside the car as Damon was swinging the bat at the windows. It felt like I was in a horror movie, you know how the villain keeps showing up and you can't get away. It was scary," said Samantha.

"Yeah, it was scary when we actually saw him going crazy with that bat. I'm so glad you and I were together and I could help you through this," said Lauren.

"I don't know what I would have done if I were by myself. And thanks again for letting me stay with you. I probably would have checked into a hotel if you didn't live in the area," said Samantha.

"You can stay here as long as you need to. I'm not pushing you out. Besides, I like the company," said Lauren.

"Speaking of company, I thought you said Charles was on a fishing trip with his friend. Were you expecting him to come home tonight?" asked Samantha.

Lauren gave a huge sigh. "Sam, I really don't know. I didn't tell you the full story, as far as Charles is concerned," she said.

"What's going on?" asked Samantha.

"Remember, I said that Charles and I had been fighting a lot lately?" asked Lauren.

"Yes, you told us on the ski trip. And you said the fights stemmed from Charles losing his job. Is all that still the case," asked Samantha.

"It is, but the biggest fight happened when I got my acceptance letter to the pastry bootcamp in France. Charles didn't want me to go," said Lauren. "He said if I went that he would not be here when I returned."

"Oh no …" said Samantha.

"I didn't believe him, but it seems he was telling the

truth. I haven't seen or heard from him since I left for Paris," said Lauren. "I don't know what to do, and now that I'm pregnant, it's only going to make matters worse."

"Oh honey, I'm so sorry to hear this. Why didn't you say something before now," asked Samantha.

"I don't know … probably my pride," said Lauren. "I can't believe all of this is happening to me. The only good thing is the baby. I've wanted a baby for a long time, but Charles was never ready to try and start a family."

"Where do you think Charles is," asked Samantha. "Are you sure he's all right?"

"I don't have the slightest clue. I know he took out half of our savings. I feel like my marriage is coming to an end. Technically, we have been separated for the past 6 weeks, so I might get served with divorce papers one of these days," Lauren said sounding depressed.

"Have you called any of his family members?" asked Samantha.

"No, I'm too embarrassed. This is the first time that I haven't talked to my in-laws for Christmas or the New Year," said Lauren. "But you know what? It just hit me, they haven't called me either! They must know that Charles and I are not together."

"Hmm, probably so. What did you tell your parents?" asked Samantha.

"NOTHING! The less they know the better. I lucked up this year because mom and dad went away for the holidays. I'll break the news to them once I have a better sense of what's going on," said Lauren. "For now they are happy with my weekly phone calls to check-in. Plus, they are really busy with my dad's political race to be too concerned about me."

"I didn't know your father was running for a political office," exclaimed Samantha.

"I'll tell you about it some other time. We were not supposed to be spending so much time talking about me anyway," chuckled Lauren.

"It's ok and it sounded like you needed to talk," said Samantha. "Besides talking about you helped me to calm down. Now, I don't feel so bad since I'm not the only one dealing with drama."

"You ain't never lied," said Lauren. "Trouble on top of trouble."

"Listen, I'm going to get my water and try to go back to sleep. I have a big meeting tomorrow that I can't be late for," said Samantha.

"Ok, I'll see you in the morning," said Lauren. "Sweet dreams."

"Thanks, let's hope my nightmare has come to an end for good," smiled Samantha.

CHAPTER FOURTEEN

"Officer, I only have five minutes or I will be late for my meeting. Please, please, please, don't give me a ticket," pleaded Samantha.

"Ma'am, you should have left your house earlier, so you would not be in this predicament," replied the policeman. "Now, I have to run your tags because you were 20 miles over the speed limit."

As the officer walked away, Samantha sighed and fought back tears. This is sooo not a good way to start off the day. Amy is going to kill me. I better call and tell them that I am running late.

"Hi Darcy, it's me. Would you let Amy know that I am on my way, but I'm running a few minutes behind."

"Sure, I'll tell her. Is there anything else you want to add? You know Amy's going to ask me how far away you are," said Darcy.

"Just let her know that I am stuck because of traffic. I'll get there as soon as I can, hopefully in the next 15-20 minutes," replied Samantha. "Oh, I've got to go. I see the police."

Samantha watched the police officer walk back toward her car and hoped that the ticket would not be too high.

"Ma'am, today is your lucky day. There was some type of glitch when I ran the tags and it would not print out a ticket. So, I'm going to let you go with a verbal warning. You make sure you slow down, and next time leave enough time to get to your destination," the officer said with raised eyebrows.

"Yes sir," said Samantha. "Thank you!"

She took her license and registration back from the officer and headed off to her meeting. Well, that little episode only set her back about 10 minutes, so she wasn't going to be as late as she thought. Luck must have been on her side because she caught every green light the rest of the way to the office.

"I'm here," Samantha told Darcy as she burst through the front door with a shopping bag full of bagels, muffins and coffee for the meeting. "Have our clients arrived yet?"

"No, you are in luck. They called and said they were running a few minutes behind, too. Maybe they were caught in that same traffic jam as you," said Darcy with a knowing look.

"Yeah, maybe," mumbled Samantha. "Here take the food and drinks and set them in the conference room. I'll just put my stuff down and go see Amy."

Samantha walked into her office and hung up her coat. She looked in the mirror and combed through her flyaway hair and freshened up her makeup. Even though she didn't feel like it, she looked good with her plum colored top, dark gray slacks with plum pinstripes, matching heels and beautiful beaded jewelry. By looking at her appearance, no one would have believed the ordeal she had been through lately.

There was a short knock on the door and then it opened and Amy entered the room. "Good morning Sam."

"Hi Amy, I'm so sorry I was running late," replied Samantha. "I know you wanted to meet before our guests arrived."

"Yes, we can talk about that later," Amy said drily. "For now, let's discuss the details for this meeting.

Amy and Samantha strategized for about 15 minutes about the meeting. This was a potential client that Samantha had courted for the company and she had the lead on making the formal presentation, but Amy would close the deal.

Amy was a southern belle from Kentucky. However, for all of her charm, she was as tough as a pit bull. People sometimes mistook her petite frame and pageant beauty as someone who was a pushover, but they were always in for a rude awakening. Samantha never got tired of watching Amy charm clients and then display her steely demeanor when it was time to discuss the business details. Samantha was still learning to make that transition smooth and Amy was coaching her along the way.

Darcy knocked on the door and let them know that their guests had arrived. Samantha and Amy went to the conference room to greet the owners of J. Brown's Taste of Home. Samantha knew the co-owner and executive chef Jonathan Brown, but not his business partner Jeremy.

"Gentleman, thank you for coming. Let me introduce Amy LeHigh, who is the owner of LeHigh Creative Interior Designs," said Samantha. Both Jonathan and Jeffrey shook hands with Amy.

"And Sam, let me formally introduce my business partner to you. Ladies, I am the creative genius and Jeremy is the bean counter. He keeps the business operating in the black," Jonathan shared with a laugh.

As everyone exchanged pleasantries, Samantha lingered on her contact with Jeremy as they shook hands. There was something in his eyes that made her want to run straight out of the building. Samantha tried to push those thoughts to the back of her mind, so that they could get going with the meeting. In fact, she felt Amy giving her a small glare.

"Well, grab some coffee and a pastry and we'll get started," said Samantha with a bit of a shaky voice. She didn't usually get nervous. I don't know what kind of voodoo Jeremy was putting on her with those piercing blue eyes, but he better stop it right now!

Samantha pulled herself together and started the presentation about J. Brown's Taste of Home. This was the first restaurant they were opening in Baltimore, Maryland and they wanted it to have a different ambiance than the other two locations. J. Brown's was an upscale soul food restaurant and the décor needed to capture class, style and comfort, but with chic urban flair.

Both Jeremy and Jonathan seemed to like the themes and concepts that she had come up with. And Amy gave an overview of the financials to close out the presentation. "Sam, you did a great job with these concepts. I love the different color combinations that you've come up with," said Jonathan.

"Of course, we need to discuss the details and I think we have one more firm to meet with before we make a final decision," said Jeremy.

"I'm sure you'll find that we are quite reasonably priced for this market and our level of expertise," said Amy. "But please take all the time you need in making a decision."

"Yes, I agree, take your time. We'd love to work with you on this," said Samantha. "I think it will be a great partnership, but I understand that you want to weigh all of your options. I doubt that you will find anyone else to capture your vision quite like we can." Samantha was teasing Jonathan.

"Ok, you've got jokes. By the way, that's an inside joke and we are going to leave it there," said Jonathan.

"You seem pretty sure of yourself Samantha," said Jeremy, who had been looking suspiciously back and forth between her and Jonathan.

"Let's just chalk it up to my sixth sense," said Samantha with a sly smile. "I'll give you a follow-up call at the beginning of next week to see if you have any questions."

"That sounds good Sam," said Jonathan. "We'll talk to you next week." The men headed out, but Jeremy came back and handed Samantha his card.

"Here you go, I forgot to give this to you. You can give me a call, rather than Jonathan," he added a bit sternly.

"Alright, I'll talk to you next week Jeremy," said Samantha. "Have a great day."

"You too," he replied and then walked out.

"Hmm, that was interesting," said Amy. "If I didn't know any better I would think that he was jealous of your relationship with Jonathan."

"Oh please, I'm sure he didn't want Jonathan to show their hand. Besides, there is no relationship between Jonathan and I. We've become good friends, almost like brother and sister."

"Humph, I know when a man is interested, and Jeremy is definitely interested in you darlin'," said Amy. "If I didn't have a conference call, I'd continue this conversation but I must run. However, I will leave you with this thought – keep things professional, at least until the job is done."

Amy is a trip! She doesn't know that I don't date white men, no matter how fine they are. So, she doesn't have anything to worry about on that front. I don't care how interested or uninterested Jeremy is, it is not going to happen.

"Oh, I didn't realize that you were still in here," said Darcy. "I just came to get a bagel and some coffee."

"Sure, no problem," said Samantha. Darcy looked at her with a puzzled expression because of the faraway look on her face.

"I guess the blue skies have your creative juices flowing," asked Darcy.

"What? I didn't notice his blue eyes," said Samantha, snapping out of her daydream.

"Uh, I said blue skies … you were staring out the window and looking up toward the sky," added Darcy.

"Oh, yep that's right. I was focused on the sky," said Samantha sheepishly. "Well enough of that, I've got to check in with my contractors at the Belmont Hotel."

Samantha heard Darcy chuckling as she hurried out of the room feeling mortified.

CHAPTER FIFTEEN

I can't believe it's 7:00 pm. Where did the time go?

Samantha started packing up her sketch pad and the architectural designs for the Belmont Hotel.

"Hey guys, it's quitting time," Samantha yelled to the painting crew. "I'm heading out, so I'll see you tomorrow morning for the finishing touches in the lobby."

The guys yelled out good night and the foreman walked over to Samantha. "Hey Sam, this place is really shaping up. I hope you are pleased with my company's work," said Joe.

"Joe, the lobby looks amazing! The owners are going to be so happy," replied Samantha. "I can't wait until the paint dries and I can add the draperies and wall decorations. This place is going to be the bomb!"

"With you leading the way, I'm sure it will," said Joe. "Hey, it's getting late. Let me walk you to your car."

"No, that's ok, I'm fine. Besides, there's a security guard out front and the parking lot is well lit," said Samantha. "Finish up what you have to do, so that you can get out of here and get home at a semi-decent hour."

"Alright, I will. Have a good evening," said Joe.

"Thanks, you too! And please tell your beautiful wife that I sent my regards," said Samantha.

As she walked toward her rental car, Samantha did not notice the dark figure in the shadows watching her. She was deep in thought thinking about the activities of the day and what was on her agenda for tomorrow.

She became startled when she heard a deep masculine voice call her name. Oh no, why didn't I let Joe walk with me to my car. Dang it! That voice sent chills down her spine. Samantha turned around slowly and came face to face with her ex-boyfriend, Damon.

"What are you doing here? I have a restraining order against you," Samantha said calmly. All the while she was gripping the mace on her key ring, ready to spray it in Damon's eyes at the first hint of trouble.

"Yeah, I know. Look, I don't want to cause any trouble, I just wanted to apologize to you," said Damon.

Samantha didn't say anything ... just cocked her head to the side and stood there studying him.

"I hate when you look at me like that," Damon said harshly. Samantha looked away briefly and gripped the mace tighter.

"Listen, I'm sorry ... I'm just frustrated. You probably don't know but ... uh, I am bi-polar," explained Damon.

Oh hell naw, I didn't know. If I had I would have kept my behind away from you, Samantha thought to herself.

"I was feeling pretty good and things seemed to be going well, so I decided to stop taking my medication," said Damon. "The police told me what I did to your car, but I honestly don't remember losing it like that."

"Wow, really? Are you back on your medication now?" asked Samantha.

"Yeah, I am. They put me on a different kind. I know you probably don't want anything to do with me, do you?" Damon asked with a sad puppy dog look on his face.

"Hey, thanks for being so honest with me. I realize that it's serious but as long as you take your medicine, you should be fine," said Samantha.

"You didn't answer my question," said Damon.

"I … think that it's best to take a break right now. You know, let our emotions calm down," replied Samantha. She didn't want to set him off and let him know that she was scared to death of him. Some things are better left unsaid.

"Ok, so we're just going to take a break for now, right," asked Damon hopefully.

"That's a good way to put it Damon. We're taking a break," said Samantha gingerly. "Look, it's getting late and I need to head to my next appointment, so I'll talk to you later, ok?"

"Ok, when do you think that will be?" he asked.

"Damon, I don't know," said Samantha.

"Ok, I won't push just yet," he answered.

"Have a good night," said Samantha.

"You too," he replied.

As soon as she got in the car, her body started to shake. She fumbled to get her key in the ignition, but finally calmed down enough to start the car. Once she got out of the parking lot, and stopped at the light, Samantha kept checking to see if Damon had followed her. When there were no other cars around, she called the police on her cell phone and reported what had just transpired between her and Damon.

The dispatcher took her report and said that an officer would be in touch with Damon to make sure he did not make contact with her again. Samantha felt some relief, but she was still nervous and jittery. She kept checking her mirror to make sure she was not being followed. This is crazy … why do I always attract the crazy, deranged dudes. I just want to find a nice guy to share my life with. Is that so hard? Geez!

CHAPTER SIXTEEN

A week had gone by since Damon had popped up out of the blue. And Samantha had swallowed her pride and allowed one of the guys from the construction team or a security guard to walk out with her when she left late in the evenings. She was finally starting to feel like her normal self again.

Samantha's phone chimed to alert her to check in with Jeremy about the proposal to provide new décor for J. Brown's Taste of Home. Oh boy, I hope this goes well.

"What's that you say?" asked Joe.

"Nothing Joe, I was just talking to myself," said Samantha. "I've got a couple of calls to make, so I'm going to head into the office. Holler if you need me."

Samantha walked down the hallway to the office and dialed Jeffrey's number. He answered on the first ring with his deep, mellow voice.

"Hello, this is Jeremy," he said.

"Hi Jeremy, this is Samantha Brown from LeHigh Creative Interior Designs. How are you today?" asked Samantha, while trying to sound both chipper and professional.

"Oh yes, it's nice to hear from you Samantha. You are a woman of your word. It's been exactly one week since we met," said Jeremy.

"Yes, it has. I want you to know how important your business means to us," replied Samantha. "Uh ... and see if you had any questions about our proposal." Now, why in the world am I stammering and feeling nervous.

"Actually, I do have a few questions. I was wondering if we could meet and discuss them over lunch," said Jeremy.

Meeting with potential clients was not out of the question, but Samantha had a feeling there was more to this request than Jeremy was letting on. She had to play it cool. "Sure, we can meet for lunch. Did you have a particular day in mind," she asked.

"How about this afternoon, if you are free," Jeremy replied.

"Unfortunately, I can't do lunch today, but I am free on Wednesday or Thursday, if that works for you," Samantha said. There was no way in the world she was going to meet with him today. She was at the hotel dressed in jeans and a sweatshirt because she was putting in some manual labor, and moving things around to make a grand presentation of the new décor to the owners of the Belmont later that evening. Oh no, when she met with Jeremy, she had to be on her A-game.

"Let's shoot for Thursday. I'll have my secretary send you the details," Jeremy said.

"Ok, that sounds good to me. So, I'll see you later this week," said Samantha.

They ended the call and Samantha's thoughts were still lingering on their conversation. She walked back in the lobby to make sure everything was progressing properly. The team only had four hours before the big reveal. As she looked around the room, she noticed that the drapery surrounding one of the windows was not flowing properly from the valance.

Samantha dragged a step ladder over to fix the issue. As she climbed the ladder, she went into auto-pilot mode and thought about Jeremy again. *I wonder why he wants to meet over lunch instead of just talking on the phone. He better not be trying to hit on me. Oh, but those eyes sure do something to me.*

"Samantha!" yelled Amy. Her voice scared Samantha so badly that she tumbled off the ladder. Samantha tried to catch her balance by grabbing the drapery, but that caused it to rip and she fell to the ground.

"Oh my goodness, are you all right?" asked a concerned Amy.

"I – I think so," answered Samantha.

"You must have really been concentrating on fixing the draperies. I said your name about three times," said Amy.

"Yeah, I didn't hear you until the last time," said Samantha.

"Let me help you up," said Joe, who had run over when he heard the loud commotion.

"Ouch!" grimaced Samantha.

"What is it? Your ankle? Your foot?" asked Amy nervously.

"No, it's my wrist. I tried to break my fall with it," said Samantha.

"Oh dear, we better put some ice on it and take you to a doctor to have it checked out," said Amy.

"But we have so much to finish up," cried Samantha.

"Don't worry, I came to check on your progress and I'll stick around to make sure everything is in place for our clients," said Amy. "Joe, will you go with her to the doctor, please."

"Sure thing, Amy," he replied. "Come on Sam, let's get some ice first and then we'll head out."

CHAPTER SEVENTEEN

The ladies were hollering on the phone as Samantha relayed the story of her sprained wrist. The Diva Pack was doing a conference call to check in on her situation with Damon. She thought it might be better to get started with a laugh about the shenanigans going on at her job.

"Oh no! Please stop, I've got tears streaming down my face," said Desiree as she burst into more giggles.

"So, would you say blue is your favorite color now?" inquired Tiffany. That question sent everybody into fits of laughter.

"Oh boy! That was a good one Tiff," replied Samantha. "I'm glad you ladies are having a good laugh at my expense, humph." Samantha knew they didn't take her seriously as they continued laughing and throwing out jokes.

"Ok, ok, let's get down to business," said Lauren over a few lingering chuckles. "So, what's going on with your case against Damon?"

"Well, a few weeks ago, he showed up at the hotel where I am doing the remodeling," said Samantha.

"What? We live together! How come you didn't tell me this idiot was stalking you?" said Lauren.

"Because I didn't want you to be worried, especially in your condition! Besides, I called the police and they arrested him by the next morning. I made sure he didn't follow me here, too," replied Samantha sheepishly. "So, basically his bail has been revoked and he has to stay in jail until the trial."

"Oh my gosh Sam! You must have been terrified when he showed up out of nowhere," said Tiffany.

"Yeah, I was shaking on the inside but trying to appear calm on the outside," said Samantha.

"What did that fool say to you?" demanded Desiree.

"Well, that's the really interesting part. He seemed like he was back to his old self, you know, the guy I fell for in the beginning," said Samantha. "But he told me that he was bi-polar and had stopped taking his medication, which is why his behavior had become so erratic."

"Girl, these dudes out here are crazy!" said Desiree. "It sounds like he was a Dr. Jekyll and Mr. Hyde type."

"Yeah, I guess you can say that," said Samantha. "He actually wanted to know if we could get back together once this was all over. Can you believe that?"

"Well, I hope you told him what he could kiss!" muttered Desiree.

"I hope you didn't! That could have set him off!" said Lauren.

"Yeah, that's what I was thinking. So, I just told him it wasn't a good time and maybe we could revisit this at a later time," said Samantha.

"But you weren't serious, were you? I mean you just said that to keep him calm, right?" asked Desiree.

"No, of course not –" said Samantha.

"Good, because you have not had a good track record with men, but this guy takes the cake," interrupted Desiree before Samantha could finish her thought.

"Hey, leave her alone Ray! She's dealing with enough through this ordeal. She doesn't need you dumping your opinion on her, too," said Tiffany.

"Thanks Tiff. But Ray's right, I haven't always picked the best guys for relationships. However, I'm starting to see that. This craziness with Damon was an eye-opener," said Samantha.

"Well, good!" said Lauren. "Now, are you sure he didn't follow you?"

"It's all about you, isn't it Lauren?" demanded Desiree.

"Hey, you would be asking the same question if she was living with you!" replied Lauren.

"Stop! Don't you two get started," said Samantha. "I don't need this negativity right now."

"Sorry Sam," said Lauren.

"Yeah, I'm sorry," said Desiree.

"Hey Sam, would you mind if I prayed for you right now?" asked Tiffany.

"What? Oh sure, that would be fine," said Samantha.

"Ok, everybody bow your heads and close your eyes," said Tiffany. "Dear Lord, we come together tonight to touch and agree on behalf of our sister Samantha …"

Samantha was trying to listen to what Tiffany was saying in the prayer, but she just felt a loving presence and tears filled her eyes and poured down her cheeks. God, I don't know if you can hear Tiffany praying, but please help me. I've made so many mistakes and I keep going from bad relationship to bad relationship. I don't want to keep choosing the wrong people or things for my life.

"… God, we thank you for providing an answer to this situation. Now, I ask that you lead and guide our sister. Order her steps and show her the things you want her to do and the people that you want to be placed in her life …"

Wait, was I just speaking out loud. How did Tiffany know that was on my mind? Can she hear my thoughts?

Be still.

What? Who said that? And then she felt that loving presence again. And her spirit became settled.

"… Lord, we thank you! We love you! We bless your name! And we give you praise ahead of time for the things you are going to do in each of our lives. In Jesus name, I pray, Amen," Tiffany said with great fervor.

"Amen," the other ladies repeated.

"Wow, Tiff! I've never heard you pray before. That was powerful. Remind me to come to you when I need to get a prayer through," said Lauren.

"I'm just a vessel. God can use any of us when we decide to submit our lives to Him," replied Tiffany.

"I hear you sis," said Lauren. "Well, ladies do we need to discuss anything else before we end our call tonight?"

The line was silent for a minute. "No, I think that's enough for tonight. I'll keep you posted on what's happening on Damon's trial when we talk next month," said Samantha.

Everyone said good night and hung up. Samantha was still pondering the prayer that Tiffany prayed and wondered if she had had an encounter with God. She remembered feeling like that when she was a little kid. I'm going to have to talk with Tiffany about this later. I need some answers …

CHAPTER EIGHTEEN

A week had passed, and I still felt at peace about the situation with Damon. I need to give Tiffany a call and thank her right now.

"Hey girl," said Tiffany after the second ring of the phone.

"Hey Tiff! How are you?" Samantha asked.

"I'm fine. This is a surprise, I wasn't expecting to hear from you so soon. Is everything alright?" asked Tiffany with concern in her voice.

"Yes, things are fine," Samantha replied. "I just wanted to thank you again for praying for me. I haven't been able to stop thinking about that."

"Oh girl, no problem! I love to pray," said Tiffany.

"You know while you were praying, I felt like God was talking to me. Does that sound weird?" asked Samantha.

"No, it doesn't. Was it a still, small voice?" asked Tiffany.

"Yes, how did you know?" said Samantha sounding surprised.

"Well, I'm not psychic," said a laughing Tiffany. "The Bible says that is how God often speaks to us, and I've also experienced it for myself."

"I must say that you seem different than you were a year or two ago," said Samantha. "You seem more calm and sure of yourself."

"Wow, I didn't realize you noticed a change in me," said Tiffany. "All I can say is that it's God. When I stopped trying to do things my way and surrendered my heart to Him, that was the start of my developing a relationship with God. I am learning what His word says about me and I am developing confidence in His word, as opposed to myself."

"What do you mean by that," asked Samantha.

"Well, you know how my mother has always put me down with her snide remarks. I have struggled with low-self esteem for as long as I can remember," said Tiffany. "But then I read a scripture which says I am fearfully and wonderfully made, and I stopped embracing the things she said about me and I started to hold onto what God says about me. I now realize that I have value and I don't have to settle for less anymore. Does that make sense?"

"Yeah, I get that. But how do you know God meant those words for you," asked Samantha.

"That's a great question. So, the Bible, which I'm referring to as God's word, is also the place to find His promises, and they are available to everyone who is willing to have faith in Him and receive them," said Tiffany. "In fact, faith is the beginning of developing a relationship with God."

"Wow, I didn't know you were so deep into this whole religion thing," said Samantha. "I mean I've always thought that God and I were cool, but I never heard that He makes promises to people."

"To me, it's not about religion but relationship," said Tiffany. "A religion focuses on rules and regulations, but what I'm referring to is getting to know God and how much he loves me … there's great freedom in that."

"So, how come you don't really drink and party anymore?" asked Samantha.

"It's not because I can't do it. I just don't have the desire to be bumpin' and grindin' or getting drunk anymore," replied Tiffany. "I don't want to put myself in situations that don't bring glory to God, quite frankly."

"Oh, so now you're judging how the rest of us let off a little steam?" asked Samantha a bit stiffly.

"Girl, you did not hear those words come out of my mouth!" said Tiffany. There was an uncomfortable silence on the line for a few seconds until Tiffany quietly said, "Sam, you have lived your life the way you wanted to for the past 28, almost 29 years. How's that working for you?"

"Not so good," Samantha admitted.

"Well you've tried everything and everyone else. Why don't you give God a try?" asked Tiffany gently.

"I'm not sure. Let me think about it some. You know my atheist folks would flip if I told them I believed in God," said Samantha.

"In all honesty, sweetie, this decision does not have anything to do with your parents or anybody else. It is between you and the Lord. When you heard that still, small voice when I prayed … that was God speaking to you," said Tiffany.

"Yeah … I guess so. I don't know though, I have so many conflicting thoughts and feelings," said Samantha.

"Ok, let's talk again next week. In the meantime, why don't you try talking to God and see what happens," said Tiffany.

"That sounds like a good plan, I'll give it a shot," said Samantha.

"Oh hey Sam, my parents are calling on the other line, hold on a minute," said Tiffany.

Samantha was deep in thought replaying her conversation with Tiffany when she came back on the line.

"Sam, I have to go. My dad's been rushed to the hospital!" Tiffany said through tears.

"Oh no, what can I do to help you," asked Samantha.

"I don't know. I can't think. I've got to go and see my

dad! I'll call you later," said Tiffany and hung up.

Well ... um, God? I've never really done this before, but please help my friend Tiffany's dad. Amen.

This is the beginning ...

What is going on?! Samantha wondered. But, she felt that warm presence and smiled. Ok ... this is the beginning.

CHAPTER NINETEEN

"Hello," Samantha finally said after scrutinizing her caller ID.

"Hello, may I speak to Ms. French?" said the voice on the other line.

"Who's calling?" asked Samantha.

"This is Lieutenant Sheppard calling about her case regarding Damon Jasper," he said.

"Oh hi Lieutenant. This is Samantha. Is everything alright with the case?" she asked.

"Well ma'am, I'm calling to let you know that we are lifting the restraining order you have against Mr. Jasper as part of the official close out of your case," said the Lieutenant.

"Wait ... what?! Why?" asked Samantha.

"Ms. French, have you spoken to your attorney?" asked Lieutenant Sheppard.

"No, I have a voice message from her but I haven't had a chance to call her back yet," said Samantha.

"Well, I'm sorry to be the one to break this news to you, but Mr. Jasper died last week in a prison riot," said Lieutenant Sheppard.

"Oh my goodness! Are you sure?" asked an astonished

Samantha.

"Yes ma'am, I'm sure. Your case is closed and you don't have to worry about that guy bothering you ever again," Lieutenant Sheppard said.

"I'm speechless ... ah, I've got to go," said Samantha. She hung up the phone and ran into the bathroom because she thought she was going to be sick. Samantha threw some cold water on her face and tried to take deep breaths. She felt an overwhelming sense of guilt. This is all my fault! I should have never reported that he was stalking me. If I didn't he would not have been in the jail or in that riot and he would still be alive!

⌘ Lauren ⌘

CHAPTER TWENTY

I don't know why Sam has been moping around the house all weekend. "Girl, what's wrong with you?"

"Nothing," said a listless Samantha, as she walked back upstairs to her room.

I can't worry about her right now, I got my own issues. Charles finally called and wants to meet for lunch to discuss their relationship. I don't know how I'm going to tell him about this baby. Every time I think about it, I start to feel nauseous. I don't know how to handle this situation at all.

Maybe I should call Tiffany and ask her to pray for me. Nah, this situation is so messed up, I don't even think God could get me out of this craziness. Oh well, let me get myself together and face this man.

As I pulled my Jeep Grand Cherokee into the parking lot, I felt my stomach start to cramp up a bit. I hope I'm not going to be sick! I don't want to let on to Charles that I'm pregnant. After sitting in the car for a few minutes to allow my stomach to settle, I headed into the restaurant.

When I opened the front door to the restaurant, Charles was sitting in the lobby waiting for me. My heart skipped a beat when he stood up to give me a hug. I can't believe it's been almost 2 months since I've seen him. He sure was looking good with his chocolate self.

"Hi Charles," Lauren said hesitantly.

"Hi Lauren. It's been a long time, huh?" asked Charles.

"Yes, it has been. I was kind of surprised you reached out to me," said Lauren.

"I know. I had my reasons, which I'll try to explain over lunch," said Charles.

"Ok. Did the hostess say how long it would be before our table would be ready?" asked Lauren.

Just then the hostess returned to her station and motioned for Charles and Lauren to follow her to their table.

After they were seated in their booth and placed their drink orders, both Lauren and Charles started to talk at the same time.

"I'm sorry, please go ahead. Ladies first!" said a laughing Charles.

"I was just going to ask what have you been up to these last few months," said Lauren. A pained expression crossed his face at the query.

"Well, when you left for the cooking challenge, I decided to move back in with my mother," said Charles. "I didn't really expect you to go to Paris after I told you how I felt."

"Charles, I didn't understand why you would say something like that to me. I mean, you know how important my career is to me," said Lauren.

"Yeah, I do know. In hindsight, I guess I was feeling like your career was more important to you than our marriage," said Charles.

"But Charles, you know that's not true!" said Lauren.

"I think I do now. My family told me I was wrong for leaving, but I wasn't listening to anybody," he said. "My mother told me I needed to go and see a shrink. At first, I refused but eventually I took her advice. It was actually the best decision I could have made."

THE JOURNEY OF THE DIVA PACK

"Wait a minute. You sought out professional help?" repeated Lauren. This did not sound like the same man that she had known for the past seven years. I had begged this man to go to counseling on several occasions, but the answer was always the same. Maybe there's hope for them after all.

"Yeah, I know it's hard to believe, but I did because I felt like I was losing control," shared Charles. "I couldn't find work and it seemed like you were taking off like a rocket in your career. I was scared you were going to leave me, so I decided to leave first."

"Why would you think I was going to leave you? Did I give you that impression? I – I don't understand," said Lauren.

"No, it wasn't you. Through my therapist, I learned that I am still dealing with abandonment issues which stem from my dad leaving when I was a kid," said Charles. "My dad left just after I got a really bad report card at school and I guess I internalized not doing well to being abandoned. So, when I lost my job and things got really tough, I transferred those feelings onto you."

"Wow! But you know your dad leaving had nothing to do with your report card, right?" asked Lauren.

"I do now. But I guess my fears just transported me back to when I was a kid and I wasn't thinking rationally," said Charles.

"And is this also why you never felt ready to have kids?" asked Lauren.

"Something like that. I'm still working through that hang up, but I think I'm scared to be a disappointment to my child like my dad was to me. I don't want to pass those feelings down," said Charles.

"Wow, this is deep!" said Lauren. "Heyyyy, I've gotta run to the bathroom. Let's continue this when I get back. If the waitress comes before I get back order the classic cheeseburger and fries!"

As Lauren walked to the restroom, she felt her stomach

start to cramp up again. I hope I don't have to do number two. That would be awful! Once inside the stall, she noticed some spotting on her underwear and she was starting to feel more pain. Oh no, I hope everything is alright. I need to get to my doctor. Let me go tell Charles to take me.

"Charles, I don't feel well. I need to go to my doc – tor … owww," said Lauren faintly.

"What's wrong?" asked an alarmed Charles.

"I don't kno—" said Lauren breathlessly before she passed out.

CHAPTER TWENTY-ONE

What's that beeping noise? I must have really been tired, I can barely see anything. When my eyes fully focused, I realized that I was in a hospital bed with an IV stuck in my arm. Oh boy, I guess I wasn't dreaming. I passed out on Charles! Oh my gosh, the baby!

I started looking frantically for the call button to get a nurse and find out what had happened. I was so distracted that I didn't hear Charles come into the room.

"What's wrong? Are you ok? Are you in pain?" Charles asked anxiously.

"No ... I just wanted to know what was going on and, and if the ..." Lauren's voice trailed off.

"Why didn't you tell me about the baby," whispered Charles.

After a long pause, Lauren answered, "I don't know. Did I lose the baby?"

"No, the doctor said that you were dehydrated and that you probably haven't been taking care of yourself. He wants you to stay on bed rest for the next week to make sure both you and the baby are fine," said Charles.

Lauren breathed a sigh of relief. "Oh thank God! I thought that ..." she started to cry at the thought that she might have lost her child. Charles came over and hugged her gingerly. "Don't worry, our baby is fine," said Charles.

Lauren cringed at Charles' thinking that he was the father, but she was too fragile right now to bare her soul to him. "When you get released from here, I'm moving back home to make sure that you and the baby are ok," he added.

"But Charles …" that's all Lauren could get out before he cut her off.

"No buts, I insist. We'll work all this other stuff out. Our baby needs both of us," said Charles.

If he only knew … but Lauren decided not to disagree with him. She made a promise to herself that she would reveal the truth to Charles when the time was right.

"When do I get out of here?" asked a resigned Lauren.

"The doctor said he wants to monitor you overnight, and if you do well, they will release you in the morning to my care," Charles said sweetly.

Lauren just sighed and closed her eyes.

CHAPTER TWENTY-TWO

"Sam! Sam! I'm home!" yelled Lauren.

"What's she doing here," asked Charles curiously.

"It's a long story. I'll fill you in later," said Lauren.

Lauren moved around their townhouse gingerly looking for signs that Samantha was there. When it looked like the coast was clear she began to fill Charles in on Samantha's drama and why she had been staying there.

"Whoaaaa! That's some story," said Charles. "So, the guy is still locked up?"

"Yeah, as far as I know. He has to stay in jail until the trial," said Lauren.

"Well, that's good!" said Charles.

"Don't let Sam hear you say that. She's been conflicted about this ever since we first went to the police station. In spite of his craziness, I think there's still a part of her that loves Damon," said Lauren.

"She needs to kiss that joker goodbye before he loses it when she's around," said Charles.

"I know. I hope she'll stay strong," said Lauren. "Hey Charles, grab that note on the kitchen counter. It must be from Sam."

Lauren frowned as she looked at the small envelope with her name on it. This seems rather formal. Lauren opened up the note and began to read the words from her best friend.

Dear Lauren,

First, let me thank you for allowing me to stay in your home throughout this ordeal with Damon. I don't know what I would have done without you. You've been my rock and I am eternally grateful to you!

A few days ago, I learned some disturbing news. It really traumatized me and I just couldn't bring myself to say anything. About a week ago, Damon was involved in a prison riot and he died. I feel like I am partly to blame for his death. The news has been eating me alive the last few days.

"What's wrong? Why are looking like you are about to cry?" demanded Charles.

Lauren brought him up to speed on what the note said and then continued to read the rest out loud.

I knew you had a lot going on with the baby and Charles, so I didn't want to burden you with my drama. But I did end up talking with one of the guys who was working on my hotel project. He made me tell him what was going on. And I'm so glad I did.

His name is Virgil and he's originally from St. Kitts. He told me that he has a family home there that I could go to and get away for a while. I gave it a lot of thought and I decided to go. I'm not sure how long I'll be gone, but Virgil will be with me, so I know I'll be alright.

Please don't worry. I'll be in touch.

Love, Sam

"I can't believe this!" said Lauren.

"That girl is jumping from one bad situation to the

next," said Charles shaking his head. "Oh well!"

"Charles, how can you be so callous?" said Lauren.

"Look, she's a grown woman. You can't worry about her," said Charles. "You need to make sure you are taking care of our baby."

"I am taking care of the baby," Lauren said through clenched teeth.

"Babe, don't get upset. I'm sure Sam will be just fine," said Charles.

"I sure hope so!" said Lauren.

CHAPTER TWENTY-THREE

After a week of being on bed rest Lauren was starting to feel a bit stir crazy. I've watched all of the talk shows and read every magazine in the house. When is Charles going to be home so I can talk to a real person, instead of yelling back to the television, Lauren pondered?

Just then she heard the key in the door and Charles entered the house talking on his cell phone.

"Yeah, I'm walking through the door now," said Charles.

Hmm, I wonder who he's talking to and giving a blow-by-blow of his whereabouts, Lauren thought snippily. I want to be the first one to hear about his new job.

"Sure, she's right here on the couch," said Charles. "You know she has to stay on bed rest, and it looks like she's doing a good job staying off of her feet. Hold on."

Charles smiled lovingly at Lauren as he handed her the telephone and whispered that his mom was on the other end. Lauren felt her heart begin to race, and her palms began to sweat.

"Hello," said Lauren shakily.
"Hi Lauren," said her mother-in-law, Janice. "I am so

glad that you and Charles are back together and he also mentioned the exciting news about the baby! I am so happy that we are going to have a new addition to our family."

"Oh yes, I'm excited too," said Lauren weakly. "I wanted to tell you in person though." She shot Charles a glare and thought about the mess he had gotten her into.

"I figured as much, but it's alright. This is the type of news you just tell the world," said Janice. "In fact, when Charles told me yesterday, I called your mother right away, so we could start planning. I, uh, didn't realize that she didn't know yet."

Lauren immediately sat up straight at that last comment. "You told my mother," she whined, as tears sprang into her eyes.

"Well dear, I thought she knew," said Janice. "I mean after all, you should be several weeks into the pregnancy by now. What were you waiting for?"

"Well, like you, I wanted to tell my mother in person also," Lauren said through clenched teeth. "You know, I'm starting to feel a bit weak. Let me hand the phone back to Charles."

Charles was looking at Lauren with concern, but took the phone out of her hand. "Hey mom, let me make sure everything is ok with my lady. We'll call you later in the week," he added. He turned his back for a moment and mumbled something that sounded like "hormones." Lauren was furious.

"Charles, how could you!" yelled Lauren when he hung up the phone. "I can't believe you told your mother. You know what a big gossip she is. I mean what if something goes wrong and then we have to answer questions from people!"

"Babe, calm down," he responded soothingly. "It slipped out. I know you wanted to wait until you got the 'all clear' sign from the doctor, but I said it without thinking."

"Yeah, you weren't thinking," mumbled Lauren. "My mother is probably livid with me. I bet you she's just waiting for me to call, so she can let me have it."

"You know, there's nothing you can do about how she found out. You – we – just have to think about how to smooth things over," said Charles. "And hopefully, she will be so happy about the baby that she won't hold a grudge."

"You are acting like you don't even know this woman," said Lauren in disbelief.

"Trust me. It'll be alright," said Charles.

Lauren just shook her head, laid back down on the couch and placed her arms across her eyes.

"I'm going to leave you alone for a bit, so you can get yourself together," said Charles. "I'll just be in the kitchen putting the food – that I bought – on some plates. When I come back out, I hope you will be ready to eat dinner."

Lauren was feeling sick to her stomach. She couldn't think about food right now. The stuff is going to hit the fan when this baby comes out. I never thought about the effect that this news would have on other people outside of myself. What am I going to do?

Lauren reached for her cell phone and sent a text to Tiffany and Desiree. She needed the Diva Pack to help her through this situation. She sent a text:

Emergency situation. Drop what you are doing! Need to do a conference call tonight, 9:00 pm.

Within 10 minutes, she got replies from both saying they would be available to talk. Whew! I don't know what I would do without my girls, Lauren thought to herself.

CHAPTER TWENTY-FOUR

After picking at her dinner, Lauren faked fatigue and went to lay down in the guest bedroom on the main level. She and Charles agreed it was best to stay in separate bedrooms until they had worked through their unresolved issues. Lauren was thankful for the arrangement, as it bought her some time to figure out how to handle this mess.

When she dialed the conference call number, both Tiffany and Desiree were on the line.

"Hi Divas," said Lauren wearily.

"Heeyyyy," they chimed back.

"Girl, what is going on?" asked a curious Desiree. "You never do an emergency call. That's what Samantha or I do."

"I knoooowwww Ray! But things are changing and my life feels so complicated right now," said Lauren.

She proceeded to tell them about the conversation with her mother-in-law. Tiffany and Desiree were listening intently to every detail shared.

"Lauren, I'm really sorry to hear about the way things

are unfolding," said Tiffany. "How do you think we can help?"

"Tiff is being diplomatic. What she means is ... what did you think was going to happen, girl!" said Desiree bluntly. "I mean of course you tell your family the news when you are having a baby, unless there's some type of secret."

"That's not what I was saying!" insisted Tiffany.

"Chile please," said Desiree.

"Thanks for your sympathy Ray!" said Lauren. "I don't know what you guys can do. I think I just needed my girls to listen. But it looks like I should have just talked to you, Tiffany."

"Oh boo hoo! You know I keep it real," said Desiree. "Of course, I'm here for you. But I don't know what we can do. Your best bet is to come clean and just tell your husband the baby is not his."

"I have to say I agree with Ray. If you are up front with him and tell the truth, you might be able to work through this and salvage your marriage. But if he finds out after the fact, it may be worse," said Tiffany.

"I don't disagree with ya'll. I'm just scared," said Lauren. "We have been getting along so well, and I don't want to mess up things."

"But your reconciliation is based on a lie, honey," said Tiffany softly.

Lauren was silent and Desiree kept her mouth shut, for once, letting her marinate on what Tiffany had said.

"Tiff, you are right. I guess I need to find the courage to tell the truth," said Lauren. "Well, enough about me. Last week, Sam said that your dad was rushed to the hospital. Is he doing ok?"

"He's doing better, thanks for asking. I'm actually on my way home from the hospital as we speak," said Tiffany.

"What exactly happened," asked Lauren.

"He had a mild stroke, but thank God, they got him to the hospital in a timely fashion," said Tiffany. "I don't know what I would have done if things were worse."

"Oh, I'm so glad to hear that," said Lauren.

"How's your mom handling this," asked Desiree.

"She's taking things in stride," said Tiffany. "We are usually at the hospital together and we've had some good talks. She told me that my dad has some important things to share with me, but it will have to wait until he gets stronger."

"That sounds ominous," said Lauren.

"I know," said Tiffany. "Her statement stresses me out. I can't imagine what my dad has to tell me or why my mother won't tell me. It's just so weird. If I didn't look just like my dad, I'd swear that I was adopted."

"Yep, it's almost like your father spit you out, and you have your mother's coloring," said Lauren. "At least, that's the way that Sam would always put it."

"Hey Lauren. How come Sam's not on the call?" asked Desiree.

"What? Oh, I guess she didn't say anything to you two," said Lauren. "She took off a few days ago with some guy named Virgil. Apparently, he lives in St. Kitts."

"What?!" yelled both Tiffany and Desiree.

"Why are you just telling us this now?" demanded Desiree.

"Well, I've had a lot going on personally, and I figured she had let you two know in her own way," said Lauren. "She left me a handwritten note and turned off her cell phone, so I don't know how to contact her, even if I could."

"How do you know that Damon wasn't released and hasn't kidnapped her?" asked Tiffany.

"Well, I know Damon didn't kidnap her because he's dead," said Lauren matter-of-factly.

"OMG! You are so wrong for keeping all of this information to yourself," said Tiffany.

"Listen Tiff, when Sam heard about Damon's death, she took it really hard. She didn't even tell me about it in person. She only mentioned it in her note, and she seems to be blaming herself. According to her, Damon would still be alive if she had not turned him in for breaking the rules of the restraining order," said Lauren.

"Wow! We have to find a way to get in touch with her. I have to let her know that she did not cause his death," said Desiree.

"What do you mean Ray?" asked Tiffany.

"Umm, let's just say I called in a favor after that scumbag didn't stay away from Sam," said Desiree.

"Oh … my … goodness," said Lauren.

"I didn't tell him to kill the guy. I just asked my friend to have someone scare Damon, so that he would not bother Sam anymore," said Desiree.

"He definitely can't bother her now! I can't believe you did this," said Lauren. "Sam is blaming herself and this is all your fault."

"Look, I didn't make the guy go ballistic! Let's put the blame where it really belongs" said a defensive Desiree. "It's not my fault that things got out of hand in the prison."

"You are unbelievable!" said Lauren. "I can't talk to you right now!"

Lauren hung up the phone.

"Tiff? Are you still there?" asked Desiree.

There was another click and then silence.

CHAPTER TWENTY-FIVE

Lauren was still fuming thinking about Desiree's shady behavior. She had tossed and turned all night and barely slept a wink! Now, I have to start getting myself ready for an early doctor's appointment. Suddenly, there was a light knock on the door.

"Hey babe, are you on the phone?" asked Charles.

"No, I'm not," responded Lauren.

"Oh ok, who are you talking to," he asked.

Lauren didn't realize that she had been talking out loud to herself.

"Nobody. I was reading something from my phone out loud," fibbed Lauren. This lying is starting to become a bad habit. I've got to get myself under control.

"How are you feeling today," Charles asked gently. He was still talking through the door.

"I'm better, I think," said Lauren. "I didn't sleep too well, but hopefully that won't affect my doctor's appointment."

"Hmm ... when do you think you'll be ready to come down for breakfast?" asked Charles.

"I'll be down in about 15 minutes," said Lauren. Then she sat on the bed and proceeded to cry. Why is Charles being so sweet? He is making this extremely hard for me to open up and confess the truth. As she grabbed some tissues and began to blow her nose, the door opened, and a worried Charles stood on the other side.

"What's wrong?" he demanded.

"Nothing, it's just pregnancy hormones," said Lauren. "I'm fine. Please give me a moment and I'll be in the kitchen in a few minutes."

"Ok," Charles said begrudgingly and walked away.

Lauren stepped into the bathroom to fix her makeup and give herself a pep talk. She had to pull it together if she was going to survive the next few months with her mind in tact.

After eating breakfast she and Charles headed out for her doctor's appointment.

"Have you talked to your mother yet?" asked Charles.

"No, why? Has she called you?" asked an alarmed Lauren.

"She left a voice message for me on my phone, and she indicated in her message that your phone must be broken since you have not called her," said Charles.

"Oh brother," said Lauren exasperatedly. "She's not handling this well. I'll call her after this appointment."

"That's probably for the best," said Charles. "This is wonderful news, but when you don't share it with those closest to you it makes people think something is wrong. You're not hiding anything from me are you?"

"Wh- What?" asked Lauren. "Why would you say something like that?"

"I don't know. It just seems like something is weighing heavy on your mind," said Charles. "Do you think there's something wrong with the baby?"

"No! Not at all," said Lauren. "I guess I'm just concerned about what's going to happen with us. I want us to work everything out and for us to be a real family. I don't want to do this as a single parent."

"Aww, babe. I'm not going anywhere," said Charles lovingly. "I'm so excited about the thought of becoming a father, I can barely keep the news to myself."

"Yeah, I know," said Lauren sarcastically.

"Hey, it's not my fault my mother spilled the beans," said Charles with a slight grin.

"You are right. Once we get a good report from the doctor today, let's set up an appointment with your therapist, so we can start to work through our issues," said Lauren. "I think it might be helpful to have a neutral third party as we discuss our marriage."

"That's fine with me. My therapist has helped me personally and I think she would be great to help us work through our issues as a couple, too."

"Great! Now we have a plan to get back on track," said Lauren. "I feel better already."

Charles smiled with pride while Lauren crossed her fingers and sent up a silent wish for everything to work out.

Dear Reader,

Now that you have been introduced to the Diva Pack through this first book, I would like to hear from you. Please visit my website at www.karencheeks.com and cast your vote on which character's story you liked the most, as well as any other thoughts you would like to share on the book.

Were you fascinated by the sassy, bold and brash Desiree? Do you think she has crossed the line and messed up her friendship with the other divas? What's going to happen between her and the sexy music executive?

What do you think is happening with Samantha now that she has fled to St. Kitts. Did she make another bad choice? Has she given up her promising career as an interior designer?

And what about Tiffany, who has surrendered her life to the Lord. Will she be able to hold onto her faith when her world gets rocked by a big family secret?

Lastly, we just finished reading about Lauren's tangled web of deceit. Will she and Charles be able to bare their souls to mend their marriage and stay together as a family?

Each story is designed to keep you intrigued and to highlight how relationships are impacted by our thoughts, attitudes, experiences, faith (or lack thereof) and character. I am not an expert on relationships, but I've certainly messed up enough, been messed over, and gained and lost friends. I've built these stories around some of my personal experiences, situations I've observed from others and my vivid imagination. Through the Diva Pack series the boundaries of friendship, love and family relationships will be tested.

You'll find out exactly how in the subsequent books. Each one will feature a different lady from the "Diva Pack." In the meantime, be sure to cast your vote and provide some feedback on what you liked most about these stories.

I hope you are as excited as I am to see how this series unfolds!

Karen A. Cheeks

ABOUT THE AUTHOR

Karen A. Cheeks is a budding author flowing in her God-given gift of writing. She is also an adjunct faculty member at a community college and a full-time entrepreneur, who provides public relations services for startups, small- and medium-sized businesses, and nonprofit organizations. Karen is married and currently lives in the Washington, DC metropolitan area.

www.karencheeks.com